SOMETHING IN THE WATER

LOVE IN A SUNBURNT LAND

BARRINGTON SERIES

SUSAN MACKIE

small town
publishing

Images by Angie White - @photographybyangiewhite

Cover models - Nathan Storer and Ted (the puppy).

Formatting by Small Town Publishing

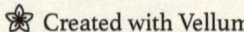 Created with Vellum

For my wicked-step-daughter Kelly,
Because your brother had a character named after him.

ANTHOLOGY - BUT NOT AS YOU KNOW IT

This novella is part of Love in a Sunburnt Land Vol 3 - but we've done it differently this year. Love in a Sunburnt Land Vol 1 was released in June 2021 and Vol 2 in June 2022.

They each comprised five novellas, by five Aussie authors - Rhonda Forrest, Louise Forster, Leanne Lovegrove, Susan Mackie and Emma Powell. Six months after the release of each one, we published the five stories as individual novellas.

The anthologies remain popular, but what we've learned in the last three years is that our readers *love a series*. So this year we're doing it differently. We're releasing the five novellas simultaneously, without first publishing them in an anthology volume. And each novella, while carrying the Love in a Sunburnt Land brand, is also part of a series for each author. While you'll find common themes within these stories, each one is set in a different region or small town with their own vibrant characters and communities.

Something in the Water is the sixth in the Barrington Series - there are three books and two novellas already released. I hope you love this story and will take a moment to explore the stories and backlists of my Sunburnt Land co-authors.

Susan Mackie

FOREWORD

While the town of Barrington does exist, it is little more than a small village with a general store, hall and school.

I've imagined elements of nearby larger towns, such as Gloucester, to create the township of Barrington for this story.

Any similarities to people, living or deceased, are purely co-incidental and a product of my imagination.

The Barrington Tops, Bucketts Mountain, Barrington and Gloucester Rivers are real, and it is a stunning region to visit.

1

'Men!' Harriet breezed into Meggie's office, nudging the door closed with her boot before setting two large takeaway coffee cups on the desk. She threw herself into the nearest chair, glowering.

'I take it this is directed at Drum?' Meggie raised her eyebrows as she reached for the nearest coffee and took a sip, watching Harriet carefully. She impatiently flicked a lock of honey blonde hair over her shoulder. After six months working together, she knew Harriet's moods. Not that she was moody, really. Just feisty and fiercely independent. Meggie admired her for it.

'Yes. Bloody Drummond Murray.' Harriet glared at her coffee for a moment before peeling the lid off. Frowning, she glanced around, the lid now laying on the desk. Meggie grinned and handed her a teaspoon.

'Ah. You're the best Meggs.' Harriet seemed to relax slightly, scooping the foam from the top of her coffee and popping it into her mouth.

'So, what has Drum done?' Meggie leaned back, watching her friend. One thing she had learned since setting her business up in Barrington and sharing the building with Harriet and Ben Evans Real Estate, was that Harriet's relationship with local grazier Drum Murray was rarely boring.

'Well. Get this. I stayed over last night.' Harriet paused, and Meggie saw a rosy flush rise from her friend's throat to her face.

'Uh-huh. You stayed over. Want to share more about that Harri?' Meggie waggled her eyebrows and Harriet laughed out loud.

'Stop it. I'm still mad at him.' She sipped her coffee thoughtfully. 'But the man does know what he's doing. You know. Between the sheets.'

'So, I now know you stayed over. You had sex. No, you had *good* sex.' Meggie was trying not to laugh out loud.

Harriet leaned in. 'Great sex, Meggs. It was *great* sex.'

'And you're angry because?' Meggie paused, 'You don't like *great* sex?'

'Damn it. Now all I can think about is the sex!' Harriet set her cup on the edge of the desk.

'The Great Sex.' Meggie tried to look helpful. 'Capital G capital S.'

Harriet stood, peeled off her coat and scarf, throwing them onto the small couch by the wall, before settling back into the chair. 'Okay. You win. I'm not angry now. But I am concerned. We need to have a serious talk. He. Just. Doesn't. Get it.' She giggled then, and Meggie relaxed.

'It's the same old argument. No. Discussion. We've had the same one since the bull sale. Six months. He wants me to move in, permanently. In fact, he was so attentive last night I think he was on the verge of. You know.' She made a shock-horror face.

Meggie shook her head. 'I really don't know.'

Harriet slid forward on her chair, then whispered. 'Proposing.' She sat back, arms folded across her chest. 'What am I meant to do now?'

'But he didn't? Propose?' Meggie was trying not to smile.

'I sensed it coming. Changed the subject.' Harriet blushed again. Meggie was pretty sure she knew which subject Harriet had segued to.

'I know we've talked about this before, but I need to ask again.' Meggie picked up a pen and tapped it against the fingers of her other hand, in turn. 'You love him?' Harriet nodded. 'You love his daughter, Billie?' Harriet nodded again. 'He loves you?' A firm nod. 'You adore his homestead and the property?' More nodding. 'He supports your business endeavours?' Silence. 'Not financially, of course. But he's always on Team Harriet, right?' Harriet nodded again. 'Then Harriet, why don't you just move in? You don't have to marry him. But you can be a family.'

'I'm glad you asked.' Harriet leaned forward, took the pen from Meggie's hand, and began tapping it against her own fingers. 'He's already had to pay out his ex-wife. Generational properties like his can be broken apart when marriages don't work. He needs to protect his assets for Billie. Re-partnering has more ramifications for him than me, and moving in full time is the same as a marriage, in the eyes of the law.'

'So, you think it won't work, long term?' Meggie finished her coffee, threw the empty container in the bin, then narrowed her eyes at Harriet.

'Nooo, it's not that. But I want him to be sure. I just think we should wait.' She sighed. 'I couldn't love him more. Or Billie.

But it's moved so quickly. I don't know. I'm enjoying where we're at. Moving in might change things.'

'Ah ha! Now we get to the actual point. Have you told him that, Harri?' Meggie pushed her chair back, then raised her boot-clad feet to the corner of the desk, crossing them, waiting expectantly for Harriet's response.

She stood, pushed Meggie's feet off the desk, then laughed, tossing her empty cup into the bin too. 'I'm glad we've had this talk. I feel so much better.' She turned, picked up her coat and scarf and swaggered out of Meggie's office into her own right next door.

Meggie called out, knowing Harriet could hear her. 'Talk to him. You're grown-ups!'

'When I'm ready!' Harriet called back.

Meggie's phone vibrated. She picked it up. Rose. She smiled at the text message.

> Girls lunch today? At Deb's? Harri too?

Meggie checked her calendar. She had a meeting in the afternoon with a young couple keen to have a small wedding, but plenty of time for lunch first. Phone in hand she walked to Harriet's office door. 'Harriet? Can you do lunch today with Rose and me? At Deb's?'

'Absolutely.' Harriet grinned, then jerked her head toward the hallway, shivering as a cool breeze flowed in before the door was firmly closed. 'The men are here.'

> See you at the cafe at noon :)

2

Turning the collar up on his shirt, Max waded through the milling cattle to the other side of the yard. He lightly slapped a heifer on the rump, moving her out of the way.

'That's the lot mate. All but two are pregnant, your new bull from Ascot is doing his job.' Max raised a booted heel to the bottom fence paling, mirroring Drum Murray.

'Yep. I'm happy with him.' Drum pulled his hat a bit lower, hunching his shoulders. 'Bloody cold wind coming down from the mountains today. Have you got time to come up to the house for a coffee? Harriet and Billie baked something last night. Carrot cake I think.'

'Wouldn't say no. Angus is covering the clinic today. I've got to drop by Laura's next, check her heifers too, but there's only a handful.' Max grinned. 'And your Harri is a brilliant cook! I'm up for carrot cake. Or whatever she baked.'

Drum said something but the wind whipped his words

away. Max climbed over the fence and began packing up his gear. 'What was that mate? Missed it.'

'Is she *my* Harri? Mate, sometimes I wonder.' Drum sounded annoyed. Not a tone Max usually heard from him.

Max wasn't sure if he should comment, it sounded like a rhetorical question. But he hoped everything was fine between Drum and Harriet, they'd become an important part of his friendship circle, in his relatively short time in Barrington.

They strolled up to the house, their long-legged strides covering the ground quickly. Of the two, Drum was taller and a couple of years younger, but Max's shoulders were broader.

Montrose Homestead, one of the finest homes in the district. Max never tired of looking at it. Close to a century and a half old, built from hand-hewn sandstone, wide verandas wrapping around the entire house, corrugated iron on the roof and four massive chimneys, smoke trailing upwards from one of them. Mid-June and already they'd had a week of morning frosts, cold westerly winds, and temperatures not exceeding fourteen degrees Celsius.

Drum nudged him and nodded toward the chimney. 'Had that one going for a full week. Warms all the rooms we use.' They pulled their boots off at the side door, padding through to the large kitchen in their socks. Drum turned the coffee machine on and pushed a cake tin and knife towards Max.

'Cut a couple of pieces while I make the coffee.' He pulled two mugs out of a cupboard, then turned back. 'Big pieces Max, we've earned it!'

Laughing, Max lifted the lid. Carrot cake with butter icing. 'You don't have to tell me twice.'

They carried their cake and coffee into the living area, by the fire. 'So warm in here. You have a magnificent home Drum.

I know I've said that before, but it takes my breath away every time I visit.'

'I am lucky. I know that. You haven't met my brother Fergus, but he's in a similar home on the Armidale property. It was built a bit later than this one, maybe twenty years or so, but still pre-1900. Our family certainly built to last.' Drum spoke quietly, but Max could hear a ring of pride in his words.

Max nodded, concentrating on the carrot cake for a moment. 'Any more of this and I'll never get to Laura's. Thanks Drum. For coffee too.' He sipped from his mug. He loved being a vet in Barrington, but almost wished he'd drawn the clinic roster today, the wind was bitterly cold outside. He chuckled. 'Do you think Angus deliberately rostered me to be out today? It's my first winter here.'

'Ha! I'm sure he did Max. He would have checked the forecast days ago and put himself down for the inside work. If you ask him, he'll tell you it's about acclimatising. I recall Petersen, the vet he bought the practice from a few years ago, doing the same to him. It's a rite of passage mate.'

Max grinned. 'But I will tell him about the carrot cake.'

'You know Laura will have something for you too. Probably lunch.' Drum raised his eyebrows. 'If you and Angus didn't do so much physical work, you'd both be turning to fat the way the women of the district feed you when you get called out.'

'Funny you say that. I turned down dinner with Meggie last week because Jill Tait had provided a huge lunch, then afternoon tea, when we were drenching there. I couldn't eat a thing that night.' He didn't add that he'd slipped over to Meggie's place anyway, after Tommy was asleep.

They picked up empty plates and mugs and walked back to the kitchen. Drum rested his rear against the kitchen counter.

'How are you going with the house-hunting Max? I thought you were close on that small acreage block behind the general store?'

Max shook his head. 'That's three places I've missed out on. Auctions, ugh. Who knew that property values would increase so quickly? Maybe I should have borrowed to buy into the practice with Angus, but at the time I thought I had enough capital for both. I could borrow a larger sum, but if we have any sort of downturn, another drought for instance, I'd struggle. I don't want to be worrying about stuff like that. I'm focussing on the business, helping Angus build it up enough that we can get an intern next year.' Max would not normally discuss his position, but Drum was a friend. Probably knew most of it anyway.

'And you're still in the flat at the Vet Clinic? It's not too small for you and young Tommy?'

'Yep. I mean, I've wondered about moving across to Meggie's. She has two bedrooms. Indiana stays with her when she's here. But call me old-fashioned, I feel I should be buying something that we can make into a home for us all when the time is right. But it's still early days.' He snorted. 'And Tommy doesn't care. He likes the flat, more so when there are animals to tend overnight.'

They walked back through the house to the side entrance, sitting on the steps to pull their boots on.

'Can I ask you something? About Meggie?' Max was surprised by Drum's words, but inclined his head, waiting for the question.

'Is Meggie. I don't know. Super independent? She wants you in her life but wants her own space too?' Drum looked a bit uncomfortable, and Max considered the question for a moment.

'There's definitely that. I truly believe Meggie and I have a future together, so part of me wants to buy a home, *our* home, with her. You know, in both names. Start our new life in something we both choose. And I don't think she's there yet. She's just started her business, it's going well, but she's really focussed on building it up. She's super smart, driven, has a great work ethic.' Max looked Drum in the eyes. 'Probably a lot like Harriet, I would think?'

'Yeah. A bloody lot like Harriet. Independent women. Wouldn't have it any other way. But mate, walking on eggshells sometimes.' They walked back to the yards in companionable silence.

3

Meggie waved to Rose, already at a table near the back of the café. Café-owner and best friend, Debbie, was sitting with her. Rose was much taller than her fair-haired friend, her hair a rich auburn. As Meggie approached she mentally noted how healthy Rose looked, her face was, literally, glowing.

'Hi Rose, you look well.' Meggie kissed her sister-in-law on the cheek and smiled at Debbie before sliding into the chair next to her. 'Where's wee Charlie?'

'Hi Meggs, Harri.' Rose chuckled. 'Kindy. He's going three days a week now. You know, so I can get some writing done.' She rolled her eyes. Charlie, age three was a renowned *handful*.

'I've ordered your usual coffees and the home-made pumpkin soup Cathy made this morning. It's so cold this week, soup and shepherd's pie is going off.' Debbie chuckled. 'We've got sourdough toast to go with it.'

'Perfect.' Meggie murmured, while Harriet said, 'Oh, good, love Cathy's pumpkin soup.'

Rose squirmed in her chair, and Meggie looked at her more closely. 'Something wrong Rose?' She laughed. 'Do you need to go pee pee?' It was what Charlie said every time Rose brought him to the cafe.

Debbie was looking across the table at Rose too. Her eyes narrowed. 'This isn't a random girls' lunch, is it Rose? Is there something you want to talk about? What's going on with you?' Debbie and Rose had been friends since school, and Meggie marvelled at how well they knew each other.

'Um, no coffee for me please Deb. I'd love a peppermint tea.' Rose pushed her chair back and stood up. 'And I do need to go pee pee.' Head high, yet with a secretive smile she strode from the table.

Meggie looked at Debbie, then Harriet. In unison, they said, 'Rose is pregnant.'

Meggie clapped her hands. 'Oh, that's brilliant news! Angus has wanted this since Charlie was born, and I know they've been trying for a little while.' She lowered her voice. 'Angus would love a little girl.'

Debbie stood up, smiling happily. 'I'll go and change Rose's order. Won't be a minute.'

Rose returned, and right behind her was Debbie with their drink order. She sat down, tried to look serious, but her happy smile was infectious. Meggie nudged her, 'How far along are you, Rose?'

'You girls! I was planning to make a big announcement, you know, like a reveal or something.' She looked hard at Debbie. 'I blame you.'

'Me? Why?' Debbie was laughing.

'You know me too well. And I struggled with coffee when I was pregnant with Charlie. I can't keep anything from you!' Rose reached across, picked up her peppermint tea, smiling over the rim at Debbie. Meggie sat back, watching the interactions. She adored Rose and had never seen Angus so happy. Harriet had become her best friend and business collaborator. And Deb. Well, Deb was just about the nicest human being in the whole town.

'Does Angus know?' Harriet made room for the tray of soup and toast Cathy brought to the table.

'He knew before me.' Rose paused, waiting for Cathy to place the meals down and return to the kitchen. 'You know, we've been trying for a little while. I fell so easily with Charlie.'

'Accidentally easily.' Debbie laughed out loud.

'Best accident ever.' Meggie chimed in.

'Do you want to hear this or not?' Rose stuck out her bottom lip.

'Go on, Rose.' Debbie wagged a finger at her. 'You're only getting away with this because you're pregnant.'

'It was the night Angus came home late after the big muster out at Copeland. He was exhausted. I'd kept some dinner for him, but he just wanted a long hot bath. He'd taken a kick to the hip, was limping badly. So, I fixed him a bath while he ate some of his dinner.'

'Mmm hmm. I think I can see where this is going.' Meggie looked across at Harriet, who was laughing quietly.

'When he got in the bath, you know, soaked his sore hip, I offered to wash his back.' Rose looked at each of them in turn. 'And....'

'And?' Debbie took a bite of sourdough, eyebrows raised.

'And it was easier to, you know, get in with him.' Rose grinned. 'In my defence, it's a very big bathtub.'

'Oh, we know.' Debbie pushed Rose's bowl closer to her. 'Eat. So, you made Charlie Version Two in the bath?'

'No. At least I don't think so. But we lay there talking. Relaxing together until the water began to cool. Then we wrapped up in big towels and went to bed. I didn't even do the dishes. He was so tired, I thought he'd go to sleep straight away.' She paused. 'I was just drifting off when, um, he started. And, well, you know.' Rose flushed and took a mouthful of soup.

'I'm getting a picture here Rose, that I'm not sure I want in my head. Angus is my *brother*.' Meggie giggled.

'Well. It was a good one. I mean, it's always good, but sometimes we rush because Charlie might wake up or Angus has to be somewhere, and you know, it's not always, um, like it was that night.' Rose blushed but her eyes were twinkling.

Meggie nudged her. 'We know what you mean, Rose.'

'Anyway. After, as we were going to sleep, Angus said, *I think we just made a baby.* And I felt that. I really did. There was such a strong connection between us that night.' She wiped a tear from her eye with her napkin, muttering, 'Damn pregnancy hormones.'

Meggie felt her own eyes welling up and put her arm around Rose's shoulders, giving her a squeeze. 'That's beautiful, Rose. I'm really happy for both of you.'

Laughing, Rose handed her napkin to Meggie. 'You better be. Because you're *fun Auntie Meggs*, and you're going to be getting a lot of *Charlie time*.'

'Great story Rose. I'm moved.' Debbie didn't look like she was moved at all. She winked at Meggie. 'But this big Copeland muster?' She shook her head. 'I've no idea. Can you tell us, without your usual long-winded-writerly-tear-inducing-words, just when you are due?'

Harriet laughed, wiping her own eyes. 'Oh, thank you Deb! Yes. The date please.'

'Let me see, the muster was five weeks ago.' Rose paused. Meggie watched her. She was happy and glowing. A small knot churned in her own stomach. What she wouldn't give. But it was too soon with Max. And despite him telling her he was up for it, he already had two children. 'I think early February.' She poked her tongue out at Debbie then. 'And while Charlie Version Two would be, er, lovely. We're kind of hoping for a girl this time.'

Harriet finished her soup and checked her watch. 'I think it's the best news Rose, congratulations. Are you telling people yet? I mean, apart from your nearest and dearest?'

'It's not a secret, but we won't be announcing it until we get past twelve weeks. But I knew I couldn't keep it from you.' Rose placed her hand onto the centre of the table, and they placed theirs over it. 'Love you. All of you. I've been bursting to tell you!'

'Love you too, Rose.' Harriet stood, glanced at Meggie. 'I'm heading back. I'm expecting a call. What time are your wedding couple coming in Meggs?'

Glancing at her watch, Meggie grinned. 'I've got time to have dessert with my Sis. I'll be back in half an hour.' Harriet smiled and went to the counter to pay.

Rose called out, 'Just go Harri, this one's on me.' Harriet waved and left.

Meggie looked at Rose. 'No morning sickness? Fancy something sweet? We can share.'

'No morning sickness, but my taste buds have recalibrated.

They did that with Charlie too. My *go to* with Charlie were these little almond friands. There was a shop near my office in Sydney.' She stopped, put her hand on her tummy, then looked up, eyes glowing. 'But that doesn't appeal at all. I want choco-late slice. Or caramel.' She stared at Debbie. 'Is this a sign it's a girl this time? Different cravings?'

Debbie laughed, standing up. 'I'm getting chocolate *and* caramel slice. We'll all share. And Rose, I have no idea, so maybe you just need to ask at your first ultrasound. Find out the sex.'

Rose pouted. 'Angus doesn't want to. Wants a surprise. But I think I'd like to be prepared.'

4

Max considered his conversation with Drum as he lay awake later that evening. He had contemplated calling Meggie to see if she wanted to have dinner with him and Tommy, but remembered she'd spoken about a busy couple of days with new clients coming in.

He also thought about the similarities he and Meggie had to Drum and Harriet. The women were in business. Smart and professional, and hyper-independent. But did that make them immune to romance, marriage and having a family? Drum had been married before. He had a little girl, Billie, who adored Harriet, and from what Max could see, the feeling was mutual. Max wasn't sure about Billie's mother but thought she had remarried and moved away or overseas. Regardless, Drum was now a single parent, just like Max.

In fact, Tommy and Billie were in the same class at school and good friends. Tommy was always impressed with Billie's farm knowledge and her confidence with horses. Max thought

Harriet had been married before too, but no kids. And she'd been through something, although he'd hesitated to ask, but perhaps he should. Ask. Meggie would know. Just to get a deeper understanding. He glanced over at Tommy, sound asleep on his back, snoring gently and his heart swelled.

As much as he loved Meggie already, he and Tommy were a package deal. And his step-daughter Indiana, who was with her biological dad in Newcastle, but came to Barrington some weekends and school holidays. But that had been no problem with Meggie from the start. Tommy adored her, and Indiana looked to her as a sort of cool older sister. His kids knew he was ... what? In a relationship with Meggie? Romancing her? Yet they only spent a night or two together each week. They had dinner, sometimes at Meggie's and sometimes at the local pub, but the only *alone* time they got was when Tommy was asleep, and Max returned to Meggie's bed, leaving again before Tommy woke in the morning. They weren't hiding it, exactly, but it was awkward.

Max knew the next logical step was to ask Meggie to make a home with him, with room for Tommy and Indiana. Meggie's apartment was larger than his little flat at the vet clinic, but she still only had two bedrooms. And it was rented. But the location was right across the road from the vet clinic, and her business was just a few doors along, so it suited her right now. Truth be told, he wasn't sure she was ready to commit completely to him and his kids. She'd been hurt before and he wanted to take his time, romance her, show her she could trust him. But was he going too slow? Max shook his head. Maybe he was overthinking. But then he heard Drum's words again, 'Is she *my* Harri?' and he knew his friend was struggling too, to get the balance right. You don't find women like Meggie and

Harriet every day. Sighing, Max closed his eyes and let sleep take him.

~

NEXT MORNING, HE WAS IN THE VET CLINIC EARLY, CHECKING ON A cattle dog with an abscess on its jaw. The old dog looked brighter, but the wound needed to be drained again. He began setting up for the procedure. Tommy would be up soon, he could help.

No sooner had he thought the words than nine-year-old Tommy bounded into the room, already in his school uniform, although his shirt was untucked and his light brown hair a mess. 'Morning Dad, how's old Smitty doing? Do we need to drain it again?'

Max gave Tommy a one-arm hug. 'Morning son. We do. Scrub up and put some gloves on and you can help.'

'Awesome.' Tommy's grin lit up the room, and Max swallowed a rush of emotion as he watched him rush over to the sink, pushing his sleeves up past his elbows, scrubbing up thoroughly as he'd been taught. Max loved his enthusiasm. He'd already declared he'd be a vet one day too.

The procedure was finished as Angus arrived. 'Morning, men.' Max watched Angus turn directly to Tommy. 'How's our patient this morning? Did we have to drain the abscess again?'

Tommy drew himself up to his full height and looked seriously at Angus. 'We did, but we think it might begin to heal properly now. We've given Smitty antibiotics too.'

'Excellent work Tommy. Now we're one patient ahead before we open the clinic. I don't know how I managed before you came.' Angus looked at Max over Tommy's head, grinning.

Max nodded to his partner. Working with Angus, buying into the practice, was the best decision he'd ever made. It felt like a family business, and Tommy was thriving. At home, in school and in recovery from his mother's death.

Max looked at his watch. Only seven-thirty, they had an hour before the clinic opened. Melanie would arrive at eight-fifteen with her daughter Tiffany. They'd pick Tommy up and drop him to school. 'Want to have breakfast at the café this morning Tommy? You've earnt it.'

'Yes please Dad! Tommy bounced on his toes, then pointed to Angus. 'You can come too Angus.'

'Love to mate. I had a piece of toast at home but could throw down a coffee and one of Deb's bacon and egg rolls. Yep, working man's breakfast for us all.' Angus opened the steriliser, putting in the equipment Max had used. 'You might want jumpers or jackets. It's fresh out there.'

Max turned to Tommy. 'Run back into the flat, brush your hair; it looks like a bird's nest, and bring our coats with you. We'll go out the front door.' Max watched Tommy take off, one hand touching his hair as he went.

Angus closed the steriliser door and turned it on. 'Ten bucks he doesn't brush his hair.'

Max shook his head, chuckling. 'That would be way too easy for you, Angus. I'm not taking that bet.' They walked through to the waiting room just as Tommy bowled back in from the flat, the coats over his arm and his hair looking slightly damp, but still sticking up everywhere.

'Good job on your hair, son.' Max winked at Tommy as he took his coat, shrugging his broad shoulders into it.

'Oh. Yeah. Thanks, Dad.' Tommy grinned, sliding his arms into his jacket as he walked in front of them to the door.

5

'Elopements. Couples saving for their first home want cheaper weddings. A small guest list, short notice and a beautiful location because it's all about the photos. What do you think?' Meggie was perched on the arm of a grandfather chair in the corner of Harriet's office.

Meggie watched Harriet process this, then slowly nod. 'Not just young couples saving for a home. Second time around, people who did the big hoo-ha first time, or they're saving too, or would rather spend on the honeymoon. I like it.'

'The young couple I met with after lunch yesterday want to elope. She still wants the dress, the cake and a small party. Immediate family and close friends, about sixteen. She said it's about the location, places that are gorgeous for photos and suit a small group. We need a celebrant, photographer/videographer, florist, cake maker and a venue. Something a bit quirky, maybe. But I think this could be *a thing*, and easy to pull together at short notice, if we have a few venues and reliable suppliers. The good news is they don't mind paying me, to arrange it, but don't want the two-hundred-a-head-big-splashy-do.' Meggie was pleased with herself; she'd been researching costs and logistics all day. In a promotional-voiceover-tone she added, '*Barrington Elopements. Tying the knot is simple, the memories are priceless.* Or something like that.'

Harriet clapped her hands. 'Love it! You're almost there. Let's workshop that.' She leaned forward, turning her computer off. 'At the pub, with wine. What do you say? It's after five.'

'No Drum and Billie for you tonight?' Meggie stood; eyebrows raised.

'They're going to Armidale overnight, to see Fergus and family. They're taking two bulls up in the trailer. Billie is super excited because gets to see her cousins.' Meggie watched Harriet pick up her handbag.

'I'm surprised they didn't ask you to go with them. Have you met his brother?' Meggie walked out of the office, Harriet behind her, so she didn't see her expression. She switched off her own computer and picked up her bag, then looked up. Harriet was standing in the doorway.

'They asked me. And I've met Fergus, and his wife Serena. They're lovely. They have two kids a bit younger than Billie. A boy and a girl.' She hesitated then, her face pensive. 'I just don't know, it's such a *family* thing to do. I'm not sure I'm ready. If I'll ever be ready.'

Meggie stepped toward her friend. 'I think this is also a-conversation-to-have-with-wine. Follow me.' Her words lightened the moment, but she sensed Harriet carried a deep hurt. Something from her life before she came to Barrington, that she'd never shared with Meggie. Chatting over wine may help.

She smiled to herself. Having a couple of drinks together certainly wouldn't hurt.

THE MAIN BAR WAS NOISY, SO THEY WALKED THROUGH TO THE bistro area, finding an empty booth to one side. Harriet bought a bottle of wine to share, and they chatted about the elopement idea while they sipped their first glass. Meggie had been harbouring the elopement business concept for twenty-four hours, excited by the possibilities and the unique simplicity of the event structure. But she wanted to check in with Harriet, aware of how astute her business and marketing radar was.

Harriet was excited too. 'It's really about packaging and pricing, Meggs. Getting a range of options together with a reasonable, fixed price structure. A sort of mix and match of options for all items: photographer, cake, flowers, cars, venue, menus, photo location, celebrant. Even preparation of save-the-date notices and invitations could be organised through the business. And you could offer short notice elopements too. Make it stress-free for the couple.' Meggie jotted notes on her phone as Harriet spoke.

'That's exactly where I was going with this concept, Harri.' Meggie clapped her hands. 'You totally get it.' She topped up their wine glasses. 'However, despite the lower cost elopement packages, one thing the brides won't scrimp on, I believe, is the photos. Every bride will want hers to be unique and that's where we can offer a point of difference with a vast array of natural sites to choose from. But that's not all.' She paused.

'It isn't?' Harriet looked at her glass for a moment. 'Where is my friend Meggs going with this?' She grinned at Meggie. 'No. You've got me. Spill.'

Meggie leaned in, and Harriet automatically did the same. 'Access.'

'Access?'

'Access to several stunning, heritage, privately owned homesteads for absolutely unique photo shoots.' Meggie was excited, this idea had come to her just before dawn, and she knew it was the piece de resistance of the whole concept. 'Barrington Homestead. The entrance. The front veranda. The formal dining room. The orchard with the house in the background.' She took another breath. 'Melrose. That gorgeous sandstone-flagged path between rose bushes at the front. The ballroom. The stables.'

'I love it. I'm sure you can get Rose and Angus on board with their place. But Melrose.' Harriet shook her head. 'I don't know. Drum's very private. And protective. He wouldn't want hordes of strangers tramping around his front yard.'

'But that's just it Harri. It wouldn't be hordes of anybody. An elopement. Often just the bride and groom for photos. Even add in a bridal party of four or six, parents and maybe a couple of kids. At most it would be a dozen. And I'm thinking, just-for-the-photos. We have the reception, whatever shape that takes, in a small local venue catered by locals. But the photos. Wow! Unless they were local, family to Rose or Drum for instance, they'd never have the opportunity to shoot those special wedding pics at either homestead. One hundred and fifty years of history, each of them. And *private* access can only be given through our business.' Meggie chugged down her wine and pushed the glass across to Harriet for a refill. 'And your cottage Harri. It's so gorgeous and quaint. The creek runs behind it.

Can you imagine shots there just before dusk, with the Barrington Tops looming in the background? And the perfect thing is, there's not much styling to do. Even if Drum only lets us use the front veranda, for example. It would be great to get photos inside his hallway, but even without that, we're talking a unique experience that most people can't *buy*. Could never buy.'

Meggie sat back. She knew she was flushed from the wine and the excitement of sharing her idea. Harriet was frowning slightly, looking into her glass. Meggie nibbled her bottom lip. Maybe there was a flaw in her plan that she hadn't thought of. She waited. Harriet looked up, cocked her head on a slight angle, then grinned.

'This is good Meggie. Better than good. It's brilliant! Very few people could offer access to these homesteads, even my cottage. And you're right, low numbers equal very little impact on the properties. And if they're not hosting the actual wedding, it's also very little time. An hour. Two hours tops. And the photos for the couple. They may have saved money on their wedding, but their photos and memories will be priceless.'

'And that's just it Harri. Even if we did one a week, for forty weeks of the year, and split these between the two homesteads and your cottage, you're looking at maybe a dozen times at each place.' Meggie stopped, and muttered, 'what if?'

'What if what?' Harriet's eyes were shining too, and she topped their glasses up, then looked at the empty bottle. 'We need to order food, Meggs.'

'Food, yes, we will. Order something.' Meggie was on a roll now. 'But what if we had other heritage-style places? The whole town is a photographer's dream. The park, the river. Even my flat over the post office. Clever picture in the downstairs doorway, another near the bakery. The bride running toward the river, laughing over her shoulder, throwing her bouquet back at the camera. Can you picture it? Low cost to put together, and we can create stunning images, unique for each couple.'

'Even the old bank building, have you seen the rosewood stairs going up to Douglas Barlow's rooms? The bride sitting on those stairs halfway up, the groom at the bottom leaning on the door jamb. I can picture it. Oh gosh, Meggie, this is brilliant.' Harriet stood. 'I'm ordering. It's schnitty night, want one?'

'Yes please. I'll get another bottle of wine while you order food.' Meggie slid out from the booth. 'You know you're going to have to sleep over in my spare room tonight, right? I want to note these ideas down, and you shouldn't drive home.' She waggled her eyebrows. 'I have Baileys and chocolates.'

Harriet thew her head back and laughed. 'I'm in. But I'm not sure how much brainstorming we'll get done if we drink another bottle of wine.'

6

Friday night, pizza night. Tommy's favourite, unless they went to the pub for a meal. Max considered their living arrangement for about the hundredth time in the last couple of weeks. It really was time he provided a proper home for Tommy. He should be teaching him the basics of cooking and cleaning and give him his own room. Here in the flat behind the clinic, they were able to make breakfast and lunch, but cooking dinner needed to be air-fryer-or-microwave-ready. So, they ate dinner out at the pub or ordered in several nights a week.

There were two things stopping Max from moving forward. The first was the lack of suitable properties in his price range, but he knew he could leverage more borrowings if he really needed to. But the second thing was what really held him back. Meggie. He loved her, was sure she loved him too. But he could see she wasn't ready to take the next step. She was working hard on her new business, which he totally understood. He grinned.

He'd spoken to her just after five, and she was breathless with excitement about a new angle to her business she was discussing with Harriet over dinner at the pub. He was happy for her and hid his disappointment that she had plans. He'd intended to ask if she wanted to have a pub dinner with him and Tommy. But they'd arranged to meet at the café for breakfast the next morning instead.

Tommy appeared from the bathroom, hair wet, pyjama bottoms and an old sweatshirt on. 'Is the pizza here yet, Dad? I'm starving!'

'Another five minutes, mate. You get set up there and find the footy channel.' Max watched Tommy bring over the small table they used closer to the sofa, then he switched the television on, already set for the football, which was starting in a few minutes. Max took over a couple of plates and a roll of paper-towel.

He'd barely set the items down when there was a knock on the door. Tommy jumped up, but Max held up his hand. 'I'll get the pizza.'

TWO HOURS LATER, THEY'D WATCHED THE FOOTBALL GAME, THEN an episode of Survivor, although Tommy was disappointed when his favourite contestant was booted off the island. Max folded out the sofa while Tommy brushed his teeth. He'd transitioned from co-sleeping with Max months ago. Thankfully, when Angus found out, he'd quickly offered to exchange the original sofa for one with a pull-out bed. Tommy no longer had nightmares about losing his mum, and Max couldn't be happier he'd returned to the bright, happy boy he'd been before tragedy had overtaken them almost two years ago. Another reason to get into a real home. It was time. Although Tommy also loved being close to the clinic and helping tend overnight patients. But he constantly asked when he could have a puppy of his own, and Max knew he was ready for the responsibility, and the fun.

Tommy was asleep on the pull-out almost immediately, and Max quietly let himself through to the clinic to check on the only in-patient, the dog Smitty. He could have gone home already, but his elderly owner had asked if they could keep the dog one more night. Max wondered if Fred Saunders, was himself unwell. He'd check on him tomorrow.

Finished with Smitty, Max strolled into the waiting room, peering through the blinds towards Meggie's apartment over the Post Office. It was after nine, and he felt sure Harriet would have gone home hours ago, even if they'd shared a meal at the pub. Yep. The living room light was on, although the curtains were drawn. He watched for another moment, glanced at his watch, then felt his body stir. He walked smartly back into the flat. Tommy was asleep. Nothing would wake him before morning. Should he pay Meggie a booty-call? Slipping his coat on over his old jeans and jumper, he let himself out of the flat into the side lane, then jogged across the road. No one was about, although vehicles were parked in front of the pub a few doors away, and he could faintly hear music from inside.

He was downstairs from her flat, at the street entrance. He tried the door. Locked. Meggie was security conscious. He tilted his head back; the living room light was on, and the kitchen too. Shivering now, it must be well below ten degrees, he sent her a text.

Saw your light on. Though I'd drop in.

He waited. Nothing. Maybe she wasn't awake but had just left the lights on. He'd give it two minutes. He rubbed his hands together and jogged on the spot, almost hidden in the deep doorway. Two cars pulled away from the pub, it was starting to empty out. He blew on his hands. The only part of him that wasn't cold was straining against his jeans. The thought of Meggie letting him in, taking him to her bed, wrapping her arms and legs around him, kept him in the shadows for another couple of minutes.

The door opened from the inside and he almost fell into the hallway. Light from her open front door at the top of the stairs illuminated the stairwell enough for him to see her. He began to speak, but she leaned in, pushed his back against the wall, and gave him a long, lingering kiss, the length of her body pressed hard against his. A tall girl, all her bots seemed to melt into his at all the right places. He kicked the door closed, wrapped his arms around her, one behind her head, deepening the kiss and the other on her firm ass. She tasted of wine and chocolate, and he'd happily kiss her for hours, but it was cold in the stairwell, and he had other plans.

One arm still around her, he took a step toward the bottom stair, but she pulled back, remaining by the front door, arms now folded across her chest and a sexy grin on her face.

'Where do you think you're going, Max Masters?' She beckoned him back to her.

He obliged, stepped toward her, uncrossed her arms and held them against the wall above her head, then leaned in and sucked her bottom lip into his mouth. It was a move that always inflamed her passion. She groaned, then pulled back, shaking her head.

'Not tonight, Max Masters.' She wobbled. He looked at her closely. She was drunk, having trouble standing up. Oh well. Now he would *have* to see her safely upstairs. Safely into her bed.

He grinned. 'Are you tipsy Meggie Hamilton?' He folded his arms around her again, and she nodded.

'Yup. I'm tipsy. Well and truly.' Then she gave a theatrical sigh and slipped out of his embrace, now standing on the bottom step facing him. 'But you can't come up.'

Max adored her playful side. He play-growled. 'But I need to see you to your bed.'

'Uh uh.' She shook her head again. 'I've got company.' She ran up two more stairs, then blew him a kiss.

'Company?' That threw him. He looked at her. She was wearing yoga pants, an oversize jumper and Ugg boots, with her rich dark hair tied in a high ponytail that had a sexy little bounce when she walked. She looked warm and cute and completely doable. He didn't believe her and started up the steps, but despite her intoxication, she was quicker, running almost to the top of the stairs ahead of him. He growled again, and she giggled. He began striding up the steps. He liked this game.

Another voice froze him in his tracks. Startled, he looked up. Harriet Russell was standing at the top of the steps, dressed similarly to Meggie, holding two shot glasses. 'This is a girls' night, Max. No booty-call for you.' She giggled. Max stopped. Harriet was drunk too. Now Meggie was beside her, glass in hand, and he could see Harriet was wearing Meggie's clothes, track suit pants that were too long for her. He stood stock still, not sure what to say. His nocturnal plans dashed. He met Meggie's eyes. She was laughing. He saw her rake her eyes down his body, then back to his face, eyebrows raised. Blast. Embarrassed now, he half turned.

'Leave now, Max. We have a date for breakfast, and I need my beauty sleep.' She laughed as she said it, and he chuckled.

'Goodnight, Max!' Harriet blew him a kiss and disappeared into the flat.

Meggie giggled, throwing back her glass of ... what? Port? Baileys? Yes, Baileys. She tasted of it. 'Good try Max. Almost, but not quite.' She stepped toward the open doorway, but he bounded up the stairs again, pulled her hard against him, letting her feel how badly he wanted her, kissed her deeply, then stepped back. She wobbled, her mouth parted, breathing heavily.

'Goodnight Meggie my love. Yes, best you get some sleep now.' He hummed a little tune as he jogged back down the stairs.

'Oh, Max?' She looked down at him, her eyes half closed, hair messy, lips parted. It was all he could do to stay where he was.

'Yes, Meggie.' He badly needed to adjust the front of his jeans. He was getting uncomfortable.

'One word for you tonight. Just one word.' Her voice was breathy. Damn this woman was sexy.

'What's the word, Meggs?'

'Impressive.' She winked, then disappeared into the apartment, closing the door. He heard the two women laughing, shook his head, adjusted his jeans, and stepped outside. No booty-call. But almost as good.

7

Meggie blinked twice, opened her eyes, then closed them. Light poured in through her blinds, her head was pounding, and there was a persistent tapping outside her room. She opened her eyes again, squinting. The door opened, Harriet stepped in, then flopped face down on Meggie's bed.

'It was so much fun last night, but why did we do it?' Harriet groaned.

'I know. So much fun. But now. Not so much.' Meggie sat up and patted Harriet's back for a moment. 'What time is it?'

Harriet rolled over and brought her wrist close to her nose. She read her fit-watch with one eye closed. 'Half seven.'

'Half past seven?' Meggie leapt out of bed. 'I'm meeting Max and Tommy at the café at eight! I need a shower. My hair is a mess. And my mouth tastes like the bottom of a budgie cage. Ugh!'

Meggie rushed around her room, pulling clothes from

drawers and murmuring to herself, then occasionally saying loudly. 'Hell. Crap. I'm going to be late!'

Harriet sat up. 'Um. Why don't you just text Max? Ask him to push your breakfast back until half-past eight?' She stood, hovered for a moment, then walked to the door. 'I'm going to head home, I'll shower there.'

Meggie stopped. 'No. Stay. Have breakfast with us.' She grinned. 'If I remember correctly, we had a bit of fun with Max last night. He might blush when we both turn up.'

'Ha! It was fun. And he's a good sport. And as much as I'd love to test that again, I promised Drum I'd feed the horses and check on the heifers. He and Billie will be home tomorrow.' Harriet grinned. 'And I plan to be well rested and have something prepared for dinner. Which might mean a little nap this afternoon. But I'll pick up a coffee on the way to my car. Coffee I need.'

'Oh, me too, Harri.' Meggie picked up her phone. 'I don't want to change the time; Tommy will be starving already. I'll just do what I can in,' she squinted at her phone, 'twenty-three minutes.'

'Okay, I'll head off now.' Harriet stepped over to Meggie and hugged her. 'I love the new business idea, let's work more on that this week. I'm going to butter Drum up tomorrow night to see if he will agree to a few photoshoots at Melrose.' She winked as she stepped back.

'Great, thank you! I'm having lunch tomorrow at Barrington Homestead, I'll talk to Rose and Angus. But I think they'll be quick to agree.' Meggie walked Harriet to the door, then rushed into the bathroom.

Exactly twenty-six minutes later, she strolled into the café, spying Max and Tommy at their usual table near the window. Meggie left her sunglasses on as she walked over to them.

Max grinned broadly as she walked toward them, but Tommy hadn't seen her as he focused on the smoothie he was drinking. She was almost at the table before he looked up, and Meggie was mesmerised as he hastily set down his drink, wiped his mouth with the back of his hand, then stood and pulled out the chair beside him while beaming at her. 'Meggie, hi Meggie!' His boyish voice was loud, but it warmed her heart to see his reaction. She adored Tommy and loved spending time with him.

'Hi Tommy.' She gave him a one-arm hug and sat, taking off her sunglasses at the same time. Looking at Max, she smiled sweetly. 'Hi, Max. Sleep well last night?'

'Of course. Never better.' But his look smouldered with promise.

'Meggie.' Tommy tapped her arm, pushing the menu toward her. 'Let's order, I'm starving!'

Meggie laughed then. 'Of course you are, and I'm sorry I kept you waiting.' She picked up the menu. 'What haven't we tried, Tommy?' They'd been working their way through the breakfast options together; Meggie loved collaborating with Tommy over their meal choices.

'Let's see. We had omelette last time and the Canadian breakfast before that.' He wrinkled his nose, looking up at her. 'But maple syrup on bacon just didn't float my boat.'

Meggie snorted, then tried to change it to a cough. 'No. You're right. But I feel like something, I don't know, savoury. What do you think?'

'Deb has a special up this morning. It's a corn and zucchini fritter with crispy bacon and a poached egg and some sort of tomato relish.' He stood, menu in hand. 'I'm game if you are?'

'Okay, Tommy, I'm game. And coffee please. A big one.' Meggie reached for her purse, she tried to take paying for breakfast in turns with Max, but Tommy already had Max's card in his hand.

'Dad's having the scrambled eggs and bacon. Again.' Tommy shared a look of mild exasperation with her, and they giggled because Max rarely deviated from his breakfast of choice.

Max leaned in as Tommy walked toward the counter. 'How did *you* sleep last night, Meggs?' He raised his eyebrows.

'The sleeping was good. Deep. It was the waking up I had trouble with.' She chuckled. 'Harri and I talked about you before she left this morning.' Meggie settled back, eyebrows raised. She thought he seemed slightly uncomfortable.

'Should I be embarrassed? Can I still look her in the eye?' He laughed as he spoke, and Meggie felt her heart beat faster for a moment. He really is one of the good ones.

'Okay. She said you're a good sport.' Glancing at Tommy, still ordering their breakfast, she added more quietly, 'But if she hadn't been there, Max Masters, I would have, um, sorted your, er, obvious discomfort. Quickly.'

Tommy was busy paying and Max took the opportunity to lean in closer, his lips almost brushing her ear. 'I suspect, Meggie Hamilton, that had Harriet not been there, I may have gotten you to your bed. And that's all. There is a certain level of intoxication that would make a man think twice. And you were borderline, Meggs.'

She blushed as Tommy joined them, looking first to his father, then to her. 'What? What's so funny?'

'We were just talking about how well we each slept last night.' Max spoke in a monotone and Meggie had to look down, move the cutlery slightly, to not meet his eye and laugh.

'Really? That's so boring.' Tommy shook his head and sighed. 'Adults.'

Their coffee arrived, and she asked Tommy about school and patients in the clinic hospital. As she watched him happily chat while they waited for their breakfast, she wondered, not for the first time, why Max had not bought them a home yet. Tommy was puppy and horse mad and needed room to run around. A place he could invite friends to stay at. Their tiny flat didn't allow for any of that. She didn't think it was a lack of funds. She knew he'd sold his house and the share of his practice in Newcastle. And while he had to buy into the clinic with Angus, it surely wouldn't have left him short.

Breakfast arrived, and Tommy was quiet while he ate. Meggie watched him through lowered lids while he took his first bite of the fritter. She loved how adventurous he was with food. He closed his eyes briefly while he chewed. Meggie waited for his reaction. He opened his eyes and looked straight at her. He grinned, gave a thumbs up and cut into the egg on top. A small amount of yolk crept over the fritter, and Tommy enthusiastically put another section of fritter, this time with egg and bacon, on his fork. Meggie did the same. It was delicious. And eyes wide open she swallowed the first mouthful and gave him a thumbs up. 'Good choice Tommy, just what I felt like this morning.' He nodded happily.

Meggie turned to glance at Max. He was looking at her with open admiration. And something else. Her face grew warm. He'd never said it, but his eyes were full of love. For Tommy, of course, and yes, maybe for her. Smiling she concentrated on

her meal again. *Definitely* for her. They hadn't declared themselves, but she knew in her heart that he loved her. And she
loved him. But it was complicated. Max had to put Tommy and
his step-daughter Indiana first. Meggie wouldn't have it any
other way; and it was another reason to love him. Their time
would come.

Meggie asked Tommy how they planned to spend the day,
just as they finished eating.

'There's no footy, we've got the bye this week. Dad and I are
going to take Smitty home to Mr Saunders today, he hasn't been
well enough to drive in and pick him up.' Tommy looked at his
father, then turned back to Meggie. 'I've been helping to look
after Smitty. He had an abscess in his jaw.'

'Actually, I know Smitty too. I think he is the father, or
maybe grandfather, of Woof, Charlie's young dog. Fred Saunders has bred working cattle dogs his whole life and Rose says
her grandfather would only buy a young dog from him.' Meggie
reached for her purse. 'Do you have time for another drink? I'm
going to get a chai latte.'

Max looked at Tommy, who nodded eagerly. 'Sure, I'll have
a short black. What do you want Tommy?'

'Hot chocolate please Meggie.' Tommy pushed his chair
back noisily, standing quickly. 'I can order the drinks for you.'

Meggie handed him some cash, happy to stay where she
was. Turning to Max, she asked. 'Mr Saunders? Is he alright?'

'I'm not sure. He's been having treatment, and I think he's
struggling with the farm. That's why I told him we'd bring the
dog home today; I want to check on him, make sure he has food
in the house and see if his other animals are alright.' Max
straightened. 'Not that he'd ever endanger his livestock, but I
think his health is worse than he admits.'

Nodding, Meggie put her hand over Max's for a moment. 'He's lucky he has you to check on him. I know he doesn't have any family left in the area.'

Max sighed. 'Angus would do it too, it's just that I've been treating Smitty, and Tommy is very attached.'

Tommy was still waiting to be served at the counter. Meggie chuckled. 'He does love his food.'

'That he does. But he's as skinny as a whippet. Runs it all off.' Max grinned. 'No idea where he gets the energy.'

Laughing, Meggie nudged Max with her shoulder. 'I know where he gets it from.' They leaned into each other for a moment. 'Um, if the Masters' men have no plans later, would you like to come over to my place for dinner? We can watch a movie after, and, you know, if it gets late, you can stay over.' She waggled her eyebrows, and Max laughed out loud.

'That's an offer I can't refuse.' She loved the way Max's eyes crinkled at the corners when he smiled. And she loved the way her body tingled when he looked at her like that.

'What can't you refuse, Dad?' Tommy had bounded back to their table, now sitting beside his father. He handed Meggie her change.

'Meggie has invited us for dinner tonight at her place, and maybe a movie.'

'Excellent!' Tommy turned to Meggie. 'What will you cook?' She laughed at that.

'I'm thinking about Mexican. Tacos or tortillas. You know, mince topped with salsa, guacamole and cheese. We can put them together ourselves. And I've been wanting to try a dessert recipe I saw on Facebook. Chocolate raspberry money bags. With cream and ice cream. Want to help?' Meggie saw Tommy's face light up. Not only did he enjoy food, Tommy liked cooking too. Something he couldn't do in their little flat.

'Bewdy. I'll help you, Meggs.' Tommy looked at his father for confirmation.

Meggie watched as Max pretended to consider it, until Tommy punched him lightly on the arm and said, 'Da-ad!'

'Of course we can help. We'll come at five, if that suits you. What can we bring?'

Their drinks arrived, and Meggie chuckled as she sipped her chai. 'Just yourselves. You're more than enough!'

8

As it turned out, they didn't get to Meggie's until almost five-thirty. The visit to see old Fred Saunders did not go as planned. They arrived just before lunch. Tommy carefully helped Smitty out of their car. He'd stayed quietly on the passenger side floor at Tommy's feet the whole way there.

It took ages for Fred to come to the door, and when he opened it, he was pale and had dark circles under his eyes. He was so thin the skin on his hands was almost translucent. But his face lit up when he saw his dog, and he sat down on a seat near the door, allowing the dog to sit at his knees, where he patted his head, looking into his eyes, telling him how happy he was to have him home. Smitty's tail thumped on the veranda floor as he gazed into his master's face.

Finally, seemingly satisfied the dog was in good health, he looked up at Max and Tommy. His eyes focussed on Tommy, asking him what he had been doing for Smitty. Tommy sat down beside him, describing the operation to remove the abscess and all the aftercare he'd been given. Fred Saunders nodded as Tommy spoke, occasionally glancing at Max, who confirmed Tommy's words.

'How are your other animals, Fred? The other dogs? You have puppies due soon, I think. And your cattle?' Tommy had stood, moving beside his father as he spoke, and Max laid one arm loosely across his son's shoulders.

Fred leaned back. 'It's just the dogs now, Max. And a few chooks.' He coughed for a moment, bringing a large handkerchief from the depths of his overalls to wipe his mouth. Max thought he looked like he should be in hospital, or in bed at least.

'Just the dogs?' Max raised his eyebrows.

Fred sighed. 'I've sold off all but thirty acres. The farm was always across two lots, it's the way my father bought it. He built this house on the smaller lot, thinking he'd stay in it when he was old, and I could build another house on the larger lot when I married. But he didn't make old bones, so Betty and I lived here. Raised our children here. Now they've all moved away, have children of their own.' He coughed again, and Max sat beside him.

'Is it alright if Tommy goes around the back to have a look at the other dogs, Fred?'

Fred nodded. 'You can let the chooks out too, young Tommy. I haven't been out there today.' As Tommy sped off, Smitty trotting after him, Fred turned back to Max. 'We had a family meeting at Christmas, and it seemed best to sell off the larger lot. I couldn't manage it and prices are good. The money is safe, and the kids think I might need to move to a nursing home.' He paused. 'I've got cancer Max. It's my third bout, and

I know it will take me this time.' He lifted his chin, touching his throat. 'It's in the throat. Thyroid too. And lymph nodes. So, I won't be moving to a nursing home. I'll die here. I want to die here. And my days are numbered. But with Betty gone these last dozen years, it's just me. And the dogs and chooks now.'

Max swallowed, wanting to keep his composure. He had a lot of time for Fred Saunders and knew he needed to maintain his dignity. 'I understand, Fred. And I'm sorry to hear that.' He looked closely at the old man, who met his gaze steadily. 'May I ask what your plan is? For the dogs and chooks and your own daily care?'

Fred nodded. 'My oldest girl Sally is closest; she lives in Taree. She comes over every Friday, cleans the house and does the shopping for me. Prepares some meals. And the others are taking turns to come on weekends. They all work.' He paused, coughing again, shaking his head as he held the handkerchief to his mouth. Max waited silently. He watched Fred take another breath. 'Not that I eat much, but what she leaves me is good. And I have fresh eggs every day. Although it's been a struggle today.'

'That's my concern, Fred. Sally is doing a great job and you have someone here every weekend. But what about Monday through Thursday? If you have a day like today where you can't.' Max stopped. He was going to say, 'can't get out of bed', or 'can't feed yourself', but he continued with, 'can't feed the dogs and the chooks. Check on the new puppies?' He waited.

Fred sighed. 'I'll call. If I can. If there's time.' He shook his head sadly, and this time Max saw tears in his eyes.

They sat in silence for a moment. Max had an idea. He turned to Fred. 'Tommy and I can drop by Monday to Thursday, before and after school. It's only two kilometres further, a few minutes each way.'

'I can't ask you to do that Max, but I thank you for the offer.'

'You'd be doing me a favour. Tommy is dog mad, adores Smitty. He'll be as keen as mustard to take care of him, and the others. And the chooks too.' Max grinned. 'Maybe we can take a couple of eggs home some days, after we check you have yours.'

Fred looked away for a moment and Max knew it best he say nothing while the old man considered his words. 'Alright. You leave me two eggs each day and take the rest. I'm getting about eight most days, so there's plenty. And I'd like to do something for young Tommy, if he's going to feed the chooks and the dogs for me.'

Max cleared his throat. 'I was hoping you'd say that. Are all the puppies from the litter about to drop taken already? Could I buy one for Tommy?' Now Max glanced away. He could feel Fred's gaze on him. 'It's time I got him one of his own, he's old enough to have the responsibility. It's just that we're still living in the flat, and well, it's not big enough for a puppy. But if we can buy one of yours, Tommy can take care of it here and maybe, by the time it's big enough to leave its mother, I'll be a bit closer to moving us into a place of our own. But it can stay here, if you'll agree, in the meantime.'

Fred chuckled, then coughed again. Max waited. The old man turned toward Max and held his hand out. 'It's a deal Max Masters. And I thank you. I'll tell my kids too; they'll appreciate that someone will be dropping by on the days they can't. You're doing us all a favour.'

Max shook his head. 'It's me who's grateful Fred.'

Tommy returned, Smitty with him. 'I've let the chooks out Fred and cleaned their grain feeder. It was blocked at one end.

And the other dogs have water. I've let them into their long runs. Would you like me to feed them too?'

Max watched as Fred stood. He straightened. He must have been a tall, strong man in his younger years. He had a quiet dignity that Max admired. 'Come with me young Tommy. Let me show you what I give the dogs each day.' He walked onto the path in front of the house, Tommy fell into step beside him, and Max followed. 'Your Dad has said you won't mind coming out here during the week before and after school to check on them for me, so I'd like to show you where everything is.'

'Awesome Mr Saunders.' Tommy tried to slow his steps to match Saunders, but Max could see his excitement. At the feed shed behind the house, which was neat and clean, Saunders instructed Tommy, who listened carefully, then set about doing the jobs exactly so, his steps light and the grin never leaving his face.

Fred leaned against the wall, Max beside him. They watched Tommy together for a moment, before Fred spoke. 'You're raising a good lad Max. He'll do well.'

'Thank you, Fred. Yes, I think he will.'

9

Tommy told Meggie about the visit to Mr Saunders place, while helping her set the various bowls of Mexican food on the table, and how he would be helping to look after the dogs and chickens during the week. She loved the excitement in his voice, and his pride at having the responsibility. Max elaborated further as they made their tortillas. Tommy was quiet now, concentrating on making his first tortilla. He had it eaten before Meggie had even finished making hers.

'That one didn't last long, Tommy. You can make another one if you like, there's plenty of fillings left.' She pushed the mince and cheese closer to him.

'I'm a big fan of Mexican now.' Tommy eagerly started making another one. Meggie grinned, glancing at Max. He was laughing silently, trying to hide his mirth behind his tortilla, which was sagging in the middle, the fillings beginning to leak out.

'Watch out Max, yours needs repairs.' She laughed as Max hastily returned it to his plate, trying to reconstruct it.

'Here, take another tortilla. You need to double-bag yours.' She was laughing openly now. Tommy looked at his father and shook his head.

'Jeez, Dad. I'll make the next one for you.' He shook his head sadly, which brought more laughter from Meggie.

Two tortillas and Meggie was full. But Max and Tommy gamely ate another one each. Max had improved his construction with pointers from Tommy.

Topping up Tommy's water, she asked them if they wanted dessert straight away, or would they like to start a movie and eat it later, on their laps. She'd pre-made the chocolate money bags, but she would let Tommy help with serving, adding cream, and a drizzle of chocolate.

Max leaned back, patted his stomach and shook his head. 'Gotta be later for me, Meggs.'

Tommy nodded. 'Me too. But the tortillas were awesome!' He wiped a bit of sauce from his wrist.

'Tommy, go and wash your hands mate. We'll wash this lot up, then find a movie to watch.' Meggie loved the way Max always helped clean up. They cleared the table together; Max washed the dishes while she dried. There was a dishwasher in the kitchen, but she rarely used it. And she liked how companionably they worked together. Tommy returned and offered to help, but Meggie suggested he get into his pyjamas and set up for the movie. She'd mentioned an older movie called Sea Biscuit at breakfast, and with Tommy keen she was pleased she'd found it on her streaming service.

'While Tommy is doing that, Meggie, I should tell you that Fred Saunders is really ill.' Max spoke quietly.

Meggie nodded. 'I wondered.'

Max continued. 'His third bout of cancer, but there's little more they can do for him now. He's finished this latest round of treatment, and frankly, I think it's knocking him around even more than the bloody disease.' She reached across and rubbed his shoulder for a moment, hearing the catch in Max's voice as he spoke.

'His family are working together, someone is with him Friday through Sunday, but he's getting so weak he needs monitoring during the week too. And his animals need feeding. So, we've arranged to pop out before and after school. Tommy will check on the animals. And I'll check on Fred.'

'That's lovely, Max. I don't know Fred well, but everyone speaks highly of him. He was close to Rose's grandfather Charlie, too. Rose drops in at least once a week but doesn't stay long if she has wee Charlie with her. He's a bit too rambunctious for Fred.' She hung up the tea towel. 'And I know Jill Tait calls in too.' She leaned against the kitchen counter. 'But I suspect speaking to a man,' she paused, 'men. You and Tommy. May be easier for him.'

Max nodded. 'You're right. He doesn't want to be a burden, and he can see the pleasure Tommy gets looking after the animals. And we've done a deal.' Meggie raised her eyebrows at Max's words, and he peeked into the next room, seemingly to ensure Tommy was out of earshot.

'His bitch is due to whelp in about three weeks. Fred's exchanging Tommy's labour for a puppy from the litter. But Tommy doesn't know. He's doing it for the sheer pleasure of caring for the animals.'

'Oh!' Meggie almost shouted, then lowered her voice.

'That's the best thing.' She clapped her hands. 'Tommy will be over the moon when he finds out.' They shared a grin.

'Okay. Well, Max Masters, it's movie time.' Meggie took his hand, leaned in and kissed him softly on the lips. 'Have you ever seen Sea Biscuit?' He shook his head. 'You're in for a treat, love this movie.'

TOMMY STRUGGLED TO KEEP HIS EYES OPEN TOWARD THE END OF the movie, and when it finished, Max hustled him off to bed in Meggie's spare room. When he returned, Meggie had wiped her eyes, the ending always made her cry, and was washing up their dessert plates.

Max wrapped his arms around her from behind as she stood at the sink, and she paused, leaning into him. He spoke quietly, almost whispering in her ear, 'Beautiful dinner Meggie, and a lovely night. Just perfect. Thank you.' Warmth flooded her body and tears pricked at her eyes again. It had been perfect. Relaxed, fun and full of ... what? Family, she thought. It had been a real family night, and she just couldn't get enough of it.

Turning, she wound her arms around his neck and moved to kiss him. He leaned down, touching his lips to hers, looking deeply into her eyes, then pulled back a little. 'Are you crying Meggie Hamilton?' He raised his large hand and gently wiped a tear from her cheek with his thumb.

Shaking her head, she whispered, 'The movie. Sea biscuit. Gets me every time.' Meggie sighed. Max pulled her closer, her head tucked under his chin. She wasn't ready to tell him how much the whole night, being with him and Tommy, had affected her. How badly she wanted more nights like this one.

'Leave the dishes to drain Meggie, let's go to bed.' He spoke quietly, but a ripple of excitement moved through her body. Taking her hand, he led her from the kitchen, turning out the light as he went, before walking her to her bedroom, opening the door. She paused, this time taking his hand, and led him past the bathroom to the room where Tommy slept. The hall light was on, and she cracked the door open slightly, peeking in, with Max right behind her, one arm around her waist. Tommy was sprawled on his back, one foot uncovered, breathing deeply. His face relaxed and innocent. Opening the door further, she stepped in and moved his foot back under the covers, tucking the blankets in firmly. Tommy didn't move. Meggie backed out, her body against Max's, she closed the door quietly.

Back in her room, they stood for a moment just inside the door. Max kissed her mouth, then her throat, before nibbling along her shoulder blade. She shivered.

'It's warmer in bed.' Still whispering, Meggie began to unbutton Max's shirt.

He laughed then, loudly. 'You don't have to whisper Meggie, Tommy won't wake until daylight.' He shrugged out of his shirt, then helped her off with her jumper. 'But bed is exactly where I want to be right now.' He winked and she giggled. 'And Meggie, I can do the whole seduction thing, standing here by the bed and undress you slowly, kiss you all over. But.'

'But?' She almost held her breath, she wanted him to hold her, kiss her, make love to her. No buts.

'But. I want you Meggie Hamilton. I've been holding on to the thought of tonight for so long. I just need you naked.

Quickly. In this bed. In my arms.' He drew in his breath, undid his jeans and pulled the covers back on the bed. 'Naked Meggie. In this bed.'

The raw need on his face moved her more than gentle kisses, in that moment. She scrambled out of her clothes and slid into the bed, leaving room for him. He wasted no time, gathered her tightly against his chest, the whole length of their bodies touching. The bedroom lamp was on, but she didn't care. Wanted it on. Wanted to see his face.

Kissing her deeply, he sighed, then moved his body slightly. She'd closed her eyes, but when the kiss stopped, she opened them. His face was only centimetres from hers, and he was looking at her intently. She gazed back. She sensed he wanted to say something, and as much as she wanted more of the kissing and holding, she waited.

'Meggie Hamilton. I love you. I have since we first met. I should have said it months ago, and I'm not sure why I didn't. But something about tonight, about you, how the night went.' He raised his head, seeming to search for the right words. He lowered it, kissing her mouth gently. 'You have my whole heart Meggie. I couldn't love you more than I do right now.'

Tears threatened to spill over as she nodded. 'I love you too, Max Masters. I thought I was in love once before. But I wasn't, not like this. And I couldn't love *you* more than I do right now.' He laid his face against hers, and let out a huge shuddering sigh, holding her tightly. They stayed like that for a long time, holding each other. She mumbled into his cheek. 'Not just you.'

Relaxing his hold, he rolled onto his back, bringing her against his side. 'Not just me?' his smile was lopsided; he knew where she was going.

'Tommy too. I love Tommy so much, Max, that it almost

hurts. And Indiana. But Tommy ...' A tear slid down her cheek. He kissed it away.

'Beautiful Meggie. I know that. I can see that; believe me, he knows it too.' She just nodded. His big hand had been rubbing her back, but now it moved lower, cupping her backside, and in an instant the mood changed. Heat surged through her, and she moved her body over his.

'Enough talk Max Masters. I want you to show me how much you love me. Now! Right now!' His arms still around her, he flipped her over and used one knee to spread her legs, his whole body on hers. He made a growling noise in his throat as she wrapped her legs around his back. And that was just the beginning.

10

Sometime, in the early hours of the morning, Max woke as Meggie returned from the bathroom. She slipped under the covers and snuggled against him, his skin warm against hers. He rubbed her back gently.

'It's almost daybreak Max. Should we be up before Tommy?' He loved that she always gave thought to Tommy's needs before her own, but he felt, given their declarations the night before, that there was more to say.

'We don't have to, Meggie. He knows I sleep in here, probably gives it little thought, to be honest. If you're awake though, there's something I'd like to talk to you about.' He felt her nod.

'I'd like to talk too, Max. Let's get up, I'll make a pot of tea. Once Tommy is up, all bets are off for, ah, personal conversations. He'll want food.' She chuckled as she said it. Tommy always wants food.

'Umm, Meggs, I need to shower first. Before tea I think.'

Max threw the covers back and was standing as he spoke. He saw her looking at him, her eyes narrowed.

'Of course. Shower first.' She was out of bed as she spoke, her voice dropping slightly. 'You know it's a big old shower?' He nodded.

'And I put one of those trendy shower heads in. A waterfall shower head or some such thing?' She shrugged into her dressing gown.

'I didn't know that. But I'm keen to check it out.' Max felt himself harden as he spoke. He saw her gaze rove over his body, which made it worse. Or better, depending on your point of view.

'To save time. You know, so we can have tea and chat.' She walked to the bedroom door as she spoke, flinging her words over her shoulder. 'We could try out that big shower head together.'

He reached for the towel folded neatly on a chair in the corner, held it against himself and followed her to the bathroom. No doubt about it. He couldn't love this woman more.

HALF AN HOUR LATER, WARM FROM THE SHOWER, THEY SAT together at the kitchen counter, sipping their tea.

'How long, do you think, before Tommy's awake?' She gazed at him over the rim of her cup.

'It's almost six. Half hour at best.' Max reached for her hand, holding it in his.

'Meggie, you know I've been looking at houses. More than houses, small acreage lots. Tommy needs pets, and room to run around. And Indiana wants a horse. But I've missed out on three auctions.' He paused, leaned over and kissed her lips softly.

'I'm not sure if you're ready, with your business just taking off, but Meggie, I'd like to make a home with you. If it's not too soon for you, of course. And there isn't a property to consider, just yet. But I'd like to ...' He tried to modulate his voice, didn't want to pressure her, but hoped she was on the same page with this thought. 'I'd like to take this journey, the next step, with you. Together.' He waited.

She lifted his hand, still holding hers, to her lips and kissed it softly, her smile gentle and warm. However, he sensed a reticence. He waited as she gathered her thoughts.

'I'd like that too, Max. Make a home together.' She looked toward the window, the sun was rising, a rosy glow creeping across the room.

'But.' She stopped, chewed her bottom lip for a moment. He tried not to show his disappointment. She was unsure.

'It's alright, Meggie. There's no rush. It's just.' He stopped. 'Last night. So special. The whole night. I want that every night.' She raised her eyebrows and his tension dissipating. 'Oh yes, *that* every night would be fabulous. But it was the *whole* night, Meggs. Dinner, the movie, peeking at Tommy asleep. I don't just want to make a home with you, I want to make us a family.'

She flew into his arms, moving so quickly, he almost lost his balance. He stroked her hair, her lips were near his ear. She mumbled something. He thought he heard *party*?

He settled her back on her chair. A door closed further in the flat. Tommy was up, probably in the bathroom now. 'Tell me Meggie. I heard *party* but I don't get it?

Meggie took a breath. Her face was flushed now. 'Max, I have nothing to bring to the party.'

'The party?' He was confused. Was she talking about a wedding party?

'The buy-a-home-together-party. The savings I have, well, I've bought the car, paid the bond here and invested in the business. But Max, it's going to take me a while, a year or so, before I have a deposit to buy a home with you. Even then, it may not be substantial.' He could see she was embarrassed to share this, but it was something he'd already assumed. She was younger than he, had been living overseas and travelling.

'I'm not looking for funds, Meggie, just your willingness to take this next step. I hadn't even considered asking you to chip in, I know you're still getting your business off the ground.' He felt relieved.

'But that's just it, Max. I want us to be together on an equal footing, you know, as a kind of partnership. It's important to me that I contribute.' She met his gaze. Her independence and resourcefulness drew him to her, he already knew that about her.

'Just think about it, Meggie. I'd like to choose a home together. I understand you're not ready financially, but honestly, I will need to do something soon, for Tommy at least.' As the words left his mouth, Tommy flew into the room, his shirt untucked and hair sticking out in all directions.

'Morning Dad. Meggie.' He slapped Max on the shoulder then turned to Meggie who had opened her arms. Tommy stepped between them, allowing her to wrap her arms around him. She kissed the top of his head. Max saw his son close his eyes for a moment, before pulling back, grinning broadly.

'Breakfast?' Of course, it was the second thing out of his son's mouth after good morning. Food.

Max looked at Meggie. 'Can the Masters' Men take you to breakfast, Meggie?'

She laughed and shook her head. 'How about we have breakfast here? I can make scrambled eggs.' She nudged Tommy.

'Dad, you really need to try something different.' Then he turned to Meggie, smiling. 'Scrambled is great, I can help.'

'And crispy bacon and a hash-brown in the air fryer Tommy?' Meggie opened the fridge, lifting out a carton of eggs.

'Yes please!' Tommy was keen. Max thought if he didn't pursue Vet Science, maybe he'd end up a chef. His boy likes to cook. Or maybe it's the end result he likes.

Max pushed his chair back and stood. 'I'll slip over to the café, pick up some coffee, while you two work your magic in the kitchen.'

An hour later, they were back in the kitchen washing up, while Tommy had a shower. Breakfast had been lovely, Tommy had talked a lot about his new duties out at the Saunders place, excited to get started in the morning. Max thought they might pop out this afternoon, he knew Ken was generally on his own late on Sundays, and just wanted to check in.

'Max, I have a thought, it's just an idea and it's definitely not a final solution.' Meggie let the water out of the sink and reached for a hand towel as she spoke.

Max put the last of the dried cutlery in the drawer and closed it. He leaned against the cupboard, still holding the damp tea towel. 'What are you thinking Meggie?'

Stepping forward, she took the tea towel and hung it up. 'As an interim solution only, but would you and Tommy like to move in here? I know there's no outdoor area to run around, or keep a puppy, but we can at least start and end each day together, share meals .... and Tommy could have his own room....' She trailed off.

'Really?' He was excited. He'd thought about this himself, more than once, but wasn't sure if it would be cramping her style, didn't know how much space she liked or how she'd be with Tommy around *all the time.*

'And with the clinic just over the road, if you need to check on any patients, it would be handy.' He could see she was warming to it herself.

'I admit Meggie, I've thought about this myself, more than once. But I'm happy it's your suggestion. It's a great interim move. For all of us.' He pulled her close, hugged her, just as Tommy reappeared, his hair damp.

'What's an inter-something move Dad?' He bounced on the heels of his feet as he looked curiously from one to the other.

'Um, interim move, son. It's the move you make before you make the real move.' Max laughed as Tommy cocked his head on one side, trying to process this.

'Okaaay?'

Meggie straightened the collar of Tommy's shirt. He didn't squirm away like he did for Max. 'Tommy, do you like staying over here, in the spare room? And having dinner here too?'

'You betcha Meggie. Your dinners are terrific. And sure, I like having my own room.' He looked a little defiant. 'I don't need to share a room with Dad anymore. I haven't had a nightmare for a long time.'

'We're talking, your dad and I, about you two moving in here with me, so we can have more nights like last night, and start our days together too. What do you think?'

'Bewdy!' Tommy gave a thumbs up, then frowned. 'Will I have to sleep with Indi when she visits?'

'Nah mate, when Indi comes you can be a gentleman and give her your room. You can sleep on the couch for a night or two.' Max felt a huge burst of happiness as he saw Tommy nod, accepting the change without question. Gone was the little boy he'd been a year ago, unsure of everything. 'Go and brush your teeth and get your things together, we have a couple of farm calls to make today.' Max watched as Tommy sped off.

He turned to Meggie, eyebrows raised. 'You may regret this. He's always *on*, unless he's asleep.'

'It's too quiet here by myself. I'm sure I'll regret nothing.' She glanced at her watch. 'I'm going over to the office when you leave, I've got to prepare a proposal for Angus and Rose, I'm having lunch there today.' Her eyes twinkled. She'd filled him in on her new business concept. He could see she was on to something, and having Harriet's experience and support would be a bonus.

'Knock their socks off Meggs.' He straightened. 'So, this, us, moving in. How about next weekend, after kids footy on Saturday? If that's not too quick?'

'I was thinking the same thing. Gives me a chance to move a few things around here, make some closet space for you.' She was grinning, happy. He loved seeing her like this.

'One condition Meggie.'

His words startled her. 'What condition Max?'

'We pay half the rent and share food and utilities. I know you like your independence, and so do I.' He shrugged.

'But you don't pay any rent over there at the clinic. That's not a good position for you.' Meggie had her hands on her hips.

'We have to eat out much more than we will here, I'll save

heaps on meals.' Then he played his trump card. 'If the situation was reversed, would you want to pay rent?'

'Okay Max Masters. You've got me there. Yes, alright. Half the rent and general expenses.' She stepped into his arms. 'And every. Single. Night. In the same bed.' He was about to kiss her, but Tommy returned.

'Come on Dad, I've got everything.' He rushed over to Meggie, hugged her quickly. 'Seeya Meggs.'

Max stood at the front door with Meggie. They watched Tommy bound down the stairs two at a time. He leaned toward her. 'This is a good thing Meggie. Good for all of us. And I can't wait.'

11

Meggie sang along to the radio as she drove out to Barrington Homestead. She had her business plan and laptop on the passenger seat, as well as four chocolate moneybags and tub of dollop cream – she'd made extras the day before, planning to contribute them to lunch. Meggie was happy she and Max had taken a step forward. She was ready, relationship wise, but needed to get her business turning over regular profits so she could consider buying a home with Max, and when they took that step she needed to show the bank that she could service her half of the mortgage.

Little Charlie was standing on the top step of the veranda, one arm around his dog, Woof. He waved one chubby hand madly when she got out of the car. 'Auntie Meggs, Auntie Meggs.' Meggie got to the bottom step, her laptop satchel in one hand, but before she could take the first step Charlie launched himself at her, arms up. 'Catch me, catch me

Meggsie!' Dropping the satchel, she managed to catch Charlie in one arm, and steadied herself by holding the veranda post with the other.

'Phew, Charlie, you need to warn me! I could have dropped you!' She sat on the top step, Charlie in her lap. His hands were suspiciously sticky. Rose appeared from inside the house.

'I see our progeny has shown you his new trick?' She settled herself on the top step beside Meggie.

'I had my laptop bag, almost dropped him.' Meggie wiped her brow with the back of her hand. 'Crikey Rose, you should have warned me.'

'It's only the third time he's done it. We've had one each, and now you.' Rose nudged her shoulder against Meggie's. 'You should feel special.'

'Oh, I do. Special, and my heart just stopped for a moment.' Meggie glanced around. 'And where is my big brother when he's needed?'

'Cleaning himself up. There was a calf stuck on the edge of the dam, and it seems he had to wade through mud to get it out.' Rose snorted as she said *wade through mud* and Meggie laughed.

'Or he's gotten dirty and told you that to avoid helping make lunch, or Charlie responsibility.' Meggie chuckled.

'Oh no, he had Charlie with him. In the mud. And Woof. They had their baths first.' Rose laughed out loud, and Meggie joined in. Every day brought a fresh Charlie story and Rose told them so well. But then, she was a writer.

They got up, taking Charlie inside with them, leaving Woof lying right by the front door. Meggie put the cream in the fridge and the container of moneybags on the counter, dropping her satchel on a kitchen chair.

'Oooh, what's in the container? You said dessert, but no details.' Rose started to open the lid.

Meggie playfully slapped her hand away. 'You can wait Rose, like everyone else.'

'What do we have to wait for?' Angus appeared, hair damp, wearing jeans and collared shirt, holding Charlie in front of him like a football. 'Hi Sis.'

'Hi Gus. You know your son jumped me from the top of the veranda when I arrived.' Meggie fake-frowned at Charlie, who was wriggling with excitement. Angus set him down and he took off down the hall.

'You obviously caught him. Well done.' Angus stepped closer, lay his arm across her shoulders and kissed her head. Then he stepped back, looking at her for a moment. Meggie was tall, about the same height as Rose, but Angus was taller. Standing next to Angus made her feel small-ish, and feminine. A bit like Max did. Angus nudged her and she looked up at him.

'What?' Meggie touched her face, then her hair. Everything was in place.

'You look different.' Angus was still staring.

'Different how?' Meggie felt herself blush. Damn her brother, he always made her rise to his teasing.

'I don't know. A bit loved up.' Angus turned to Rose. 'What do you think Rose? Does Meggs here look all loved up?'

'Stop it Angus.' Rose slapped his arm, then stepped over to Meggie. 'I'm on Team Meggie. Always.' She turned to Meggie. 'Angus bumped into Max at the clinic this morning, and, er Tommy let slip that they stayed over at yours last night.'

'The *whole night*, Tommy said. *With dinner, a movie, then breakfast and everything!*' Angus was trying to imitate Tommy's youthful enthusiasm.

Meggie punched Angus in the shoulder. He pretended she'd hurt him. Then she became curious. 'How was Max, when Tommy said that?'

Still rubbing his arm, Angus walked over to the oven, cracked it open. 'Roast smells good Rose. Want me to take it out now.'

'Yes, alright, thank you Angus. But it needs to rest for a few minutes, so why don't you tell Meggie what you told me. About Max.' Rose gave him an amused, yet slightly exasperated look, that only a wife could give.

'Well Meggie. It seems Max has it bad. He even blushed, may have stammered. Mumbled something about you coming out here for lunch. Also said something about the next step or moving forward. I can't quite recall.' Angus waggled his eyebrows.

'You didn't tell me that bit, Angus Hamilton.' Rose turned to Meggie, eyes wide with curiosity. 'Has he proposed? Max? Something's happened.'

Meggie considered stringing them on for a moment, but she really wanted to talk about the new business concept too, so she decided to be direct. 'We talked last night, er, actually this morning, about being together. More.'

Rose nodded encouragement, Angus had leaned back, arms folded.

'Max wants to buy a home, some acreage perhaps, and he's missed out on a couple at auction. He asked me last night.' Meggie suddenly stopped, raised her hands to her lips, then turned to Rose eyes shining. 'Rose, I'm skipping the best bit!

Last night, Max told me he *loves* me. It was beautiful Rose, just so lovely, I think I cried a little bit.'

Rose took Meggie's hands and a tear slipped down her face. Wiping it away, while mumbling something about pregnancy hormones, Rose said, 'And Meggie. What did you say to Max?'

'Yes Meggs, what did you say to Max?' Angus still had his arms folded, but Meggie could see he was happy for her.

'I told him I love him too. Not just him, but Tommy and Indiana.' She flung herself into Angus's arms then. 'Oh Angus, he's such a good man, and I really, really love him. We had such a perfect night.'

Angus hugged her tightly, murmuring into her hair, 'He is a good bloke and I'm really happy for you Meggs.' Then he straightened and she stepped back to Rose. 'But just what did my business partner ask you last night?'

'Ha ha Gus. Not what you think. He asked me if I would start looking at property with him, buy a home together.' She looked from Angus to Rose. 'Actually, he said *make* a home together.' Meggie watched Rose wipe away another tear. Her own eyes filled up, just seeing how happy her sister-in-law was for her. And Angus, but he was always a sure thing. She was so lucky with Rose, loved her like sister.

'Really Meggie?' Rose sighed. 'That is so romantic.' She nudged Angus. 'You have a baby together, get married, pregnant again and where's the romance then, Angus Hamilton?' But Meggie knew she was teasing, their relationship was the strongest she'd ever witnessed.

'Well, that's great news, but there's not a lot on the market, it could take months to find something.' Angus was being practical.

'Actually. I said I wasn't ready.' Meggie saw the surprise on their faces. 'Not emotionally, but financially. I need to be able to buy in too, help with the mortgage, and I need another six months or so with the business to be able to do that.'

'Meggie, you only have to ask ...' Meggie held up her hand, not wanting Angus to go on. She knew that too, that Angus and Rose would help her with a deposit if she asked. But she didn't want that.

'We have an interim plan.' Meggie looked at each of them. 'Max and Tommy, and Indiana when she visits, are going to move into my apartment. Next weekend. Help with the rent, halve the food and other bills. Sleep together, wake up together.' She turned to Angus. 'And yes, I know he has free rent at the clinic, but they need more space for Tommy, his own room, and this is a step. A good step. Max and Tommy eat out a lot at night, which costs him too, so he'll save by having dinner at home most nights.'

'And it gives you a bit more time to get your business consistently earning. I get it Meggie, it's a good plan. A good step. For all of you.' Angus pulled her into his arms for another hug and Meggie was grateful. She knew she'd have their support, but hearing it said held deep emotional meaning for her.

Rose was beaming. 'Excellent. Brilliant news. The best. So happy for you darling Meggie.' She turned to Angus. 'Carve the roast Angus, while I see what Charlie is up to. He's way too quiet.'

Five minutes later, the meat carved and the vegetables ready to be served, Rose returned. Charlie had been crying and his face looked red. Meggie peered a bit closer. And kind of stripey. She pointed to a red mark near his ear. It was obvious Rose had been scrubbing whatever it was, off his little face. Hand over her mouth, trying not to laugh, she said, 'Rose. Is that, er, lipstick on your son's face?'

Angus spun around. 'What? Where?' He took Charlie from Rose's arms, settling him in the highchair at the dining table, but raised his eyebrows at his wife.

'Yes. Lipstick. The stays-on-for-24-hours kind of lipstick. Red. And eye liner, but that came off more easily.' She sat at the table, Meggie beside her, and passed the platter of vegetables. 'And your shaving cream may be empty Angus. I haven't dealt with that yet.' Rose and Angus exchanged a look of parental exasperation, as Charlie popped a pea into his mouth. Meggie giggled.

'Don't laugh. This may be you one day.' Rose stopped. 'Sorry Meggie, I didn't think.'

Meggie shook her head grinning. 'You know what? It may be me one day. And I can't wait!'

The roast finished, Meggie served up the chocolate berry moneybags, with fresh dollop cream and a drizzle of chocolate sauce, as Rose put a new bib on Charlie and wiped his high-chair tray clean. A couple of peas fell to the floor from the front of his shirt and Rose shook her head. 'Later.'

'Spectacular Meggie. This is what you served Max and Tommy last night?' Angus ate his dessert with gusto. 'No wonder the man's in love with you and wants to move in. I hope you told him you're not setting a precedent with this one, you still need to make treats for your big brother too.'

'Stop teasing Angus.' Rose pushed her plate away. 'Deli-cious. I've already put on half a kilo more than this time in my first pregnancy. I should be careful.'

'You'll be fine Rose. Just enjoy your pregnancy. Are you

feeling well? You look fabulous.' Meggie thought Rose was glowing, a picture of maternal health.

'I really am well. A bit tired sometimes, but no sickness. A few funny cravings, different to Charlie.' She smiled at Angus. 'Maybe it's a girl.'

'We'll know soon enough, Rose love.' Angus lifted Charlie out of his seat. 'How about I take Charlie to read a book or two while you ladies wash up? If we're lucky ...'

'Don't do the voices, or the noises Angus. He gets excited. Monotone. He may have a N. A. P.' Rose hustled him away.

Meggie chatted with Rose while they cleared the table and washed up, about her pregnancy, the latest book she was writing and the family history she had researched. It was always easy, with her and Rose.

Angus returned triumphantly. 'He's out. Fell asleep before the end of the first story.'

Meggie walked across to her satchel, pulled out her laptop and business plan. 'Can I talk to you both about an extension to my business? I'm really excited about it. Harriet's on board. I think we're on to something that's a bit unique.'

They sat together at the kitchen counter. Meggie walked them through the concept, and branding, for Barrington Elopements. They loved it. She discussed the range of suppliers they'd use, then began talking about the unique selling point of the exclusive photography, using Barrington Homestead, and Melrose if Drum would allow, Harriet's cottage, even her apartment over the post office. They asked a few questions and made helpful suggestions.

'It's clever Meggie. Easier to manage than enormous functions, and really niche. I'm more than happy to offer the homestead as a photo venue. Even a wedding venue for smaller ones, if you have everything organised. Maybe not a lot of pics inside, just the hallway and front and back veranda. The orchard and stables. Even a saddled horse in the background. It's all do-able.' Rose looked to Angus for confirmation.

'I have no problems either.' He glanced at Rose, somewhat concerned. 'But perhaps nothing booked when the baby is due, and the first few weeks. Just noise, you know. So Rose can rest, when she's able.'

Meggie nodded. Of course. She'd already considered that. 'And there'll be a venue fee, you know, an hourly rate for the time we're here if it's just photos. I'll negotiate if we want to hold a ceremony here.'

'We don't want a fee Meggie. Charge a fee, by all means, but hang on to it. For the business.' Rose nodded firmly.

'For your future Meggs.' Angus looked stern. 'No further discussion on that.'

'Do you think Drum will agree to do the same at Melrose. The photos I mean?' Rose looked unsure.

'Harriet is talking to him this week. Maybe. External ones only. But that's okay.' Meggie glanced at her watch. 'I should go, I need to start making room for the Masters Men at home.' She grinned.

12

Fred waved from his seat on the front veranda when Max and Tommy stepped out of the car. Walking through the garden gate, Max thought he looked better than he had a couple of days ago, more colour in his face.

'Hello young Tommy. Max.'

Fred began to stand, but Max raised his hand. 'You look well Fred. Nice weekend?'

The old man nodded, then spoke to Tommy. 'Go check the dogs Tommy, they're due for their afternoon feed.'

'Right oh, Fred.' Tommy grinned and shot around the side of the house.

'Sit for a moment Max.' Fred jerked his head at the chair beside him and Max sat. 'Sally was here for the weekend, with her husband Doug and their youngest, Samantha. She's almost finished year twelve and studying hard, so it was nice she came too. Lovely weekend.' He raised a shaking hand to his face, rubbed one eye for a moment.

'I'm pleased to hear that Fred. You have a lovely family, to rally around you during your treatment, ensure you have every-thing you need.' Max paused. 'But the best thing, I'm sure, is that they are all spending time with you, showing you they care. You raised good people Fred.'

Fred nodded, then patted his stomach. He was a tall man but had always been lean. More so in recent times due to his illness and the ravages of his treatment. He smiled, his eyes watery. 'Sally fed me so much this weekend, I couldn't eat another thing. If food alone was a cure, I'd be running around as fast as young Tommy.' He coughed, then laughed.

Max laughed too. 'No wonder you're rosy cheeked today, it's good food and plenty of it, I'd say.' He chuckled for a moment, then more quietly said, 'are you feeling as good as you look today Fred?'

'I am lad, I am. Seeing them all has given me a lift. That young Samantha, she's a great girl. She studied a bit while she was here, but we played cards together, and sat and talked. She helped feed the animals and we even walked down to the creek and back. A lot like my Betty she is. In looks and nature.' He shook his head slowly. 'Honestly Max, if I go in my sleep tonight I'll die a happy man.'

Max reached over, gently squeezed the older man's arm. 'You'll have more time with them Fred. Keep taking your meds and doing your chores as much as you can. Are they coming back next weekend?'

'Sally will come on Friday, stay one night. Jake and his family are coming on Saturday.' He slowly stood. 'Cup of tea Max? There's some sort of chocolate slice here, Samantha made it, young Tommy might like a piece.' Max toed his boots off and followed him inside. The kitchen was neat and clean, and the slice was on a plate on the kitchen table. While Fred made the tea, Max took the milk from the fridge. He saw three small meals plated up, easy to heat. He guessed there'd be more in the freezer. He nodded to himself; Fred's family was doing all they could to show they cared and respect his wish to stay in his home.

'I told Sally about our arrangement Max. She's happy about it and asked me to give you this.' He picked up an envelope from the counter, handing it to Max.

Raising his eyebrows, Max opened it. There were two pieces of notepaper inside. The first was a lovely handwritten thank you for checking on Fred during the week, from Sally. The other had her name and number and the names and numbers of her siblings, with the words *if you need us for anything, or think Dad's getting worse, call any time.* He put the notes back in the envelope and slipped it into his pocket. 'Sally's number.' He didn't need to elaborate, Saunders knew.

Tommy burst in through the front door. 'Dad, Mr Saunders, come quick! I think the puppies are coming!' He ran out again before either adult could speak.

'Go Max, I'll be right behind you.'

Max walked quickly to the door, pulled his work boots on and trotted around the house. Tommy was already at the dog enclosures, kneeling in front of the pregnant female. He looked, up as Max kneeled beside him. 'She's had three Dad, they're all alive. She's licking them, see.' Tommy pointed, but Max had already reached in, gently patting the dog. He lifted the pups closer to her side, then crawled into the pen with her, checking to see if she had finished whelping.

Fred arrived at the whelping pen. 'How many Tommy? She's a bit early, I didn't think she was due for another week or more.'

'Three so far. Dad's checking her now.'

Max gently kneaded her stomach. He didn't think she was quite finished. 'How many did she have last time Fred?'

'Six. Only five survived.' Max could feel Saunders and Tommy watching him. He gently palpated her stomach again and she reached her head around and licked his hand.

'She's doing her best. Let's give her a few minutes.' Max squeezed out of the enclosure and sat on the grass with the others, watching.

She licked the three pups, allowing them to latch on to her nipples. This seemed to set things in motion again, she lay flat for a moment, then Max saw another two tiny puppies slide out. He waited. She reached around and licked one, then the other. Their little heads wobbled as she did. 'Two more, they're alive.' Max crept in again, lifted the pups beside their siblings. 'I think she's done now.' He patted her head. 'Good job girl, good job.'

He could see Tommy was keen to get in, touch the puppies. 'Let's leave her to look after them tonight Tommy, you can have a closer look tomorrow.'

Tommy's face fell momentarily, but he moved back and stood, offering his hand to help Fred get up.

'I think this deserves some chocolate slice young Tommy, to celebrate. And maybe a hot Milo?' Fred placed his hand on Tommy's shoulder, and Max smiled to himself as Tommy seemed to stand straighter for a moment.

'Yes please Mr Saunders, but I just have to put water in for the chickens, I got distracted by the puppies.' Tommy ran across the grass to the chicken shed while Max and Saunders strolled slowly back to the house.

'You can have your pick Max. Of the puppies. But maybe

wait a couple of weeks, make sure they all thrive.' Saunders spoke warmly.

'Tommy doesn't know yet. We'll wait a couple of weeks. It's important he earns this Fred.'

'I understand. And I agree.' By the time they'd settled at the kitchen table, Tommy arrived, quickly taking his boots off at the door.

'Wash up in the laundry Tommy, before you come to the table.' He winked at Fred as Tommy gave the chocolate slice a look of longing as he rushed by.

13

Meggie bumped into Max on Monday morning at the coffee shop. Just seeing him set her pulse racing. The warmth of his smile and the way he said 'Morning Meggie' felt intimate. She reached up and kissed his lips quickly, while waiting to place her order. They stood together, their shoulders touching, and he asked if Angus and Rose would support her new business concept. She nodded happily and quietly told him, not just that, but they also supported their plan to move in together.

Max's response, the way he grinned at her, then looked down for a moment, spoke volumes. She giggled when he said, in almost a whisper, 'I wasn't sure if I should mention it to Angus today. What is the protocol? Should I ask your brother for permission to move in with you?' She nudged him with her shoulder, then stepped forward, their orders were ready.

'The only permission you need, Max Masters, is mine. And

you have it. Unreservedly.' She looked at her watch, then raised her eyebrows. 'Are you driving Tommy to school? You may need to get going.'

'I dropped him off already, after attending to his chores at Fred's. He's so keen, he was up at dawn, checking with me every five minutes if it was time to go.' Meggie watched as Max's face lit up. 'Oh, you don't know the best part. Fred's kelpie had her pups yesterday, five of them, and Tommy was there. He was so excited, and Tommy doesn't know yet that Fred wants to give him one for helping out before and after school. I just need to make sure all five survive these first couple of weeks. The last one was a bit smaller than the others. Then we'll tell him, and Fred says he can have his pick.' He stopped then. 'But we'll keep it at Fred's, don't think for a moment that I expect you to have a puppy in the flat as well as us!'

'I can just imagine Tommy's face, that is very exciting. And keeping it at Fred's, even when it's weaned, gives you an excuse to continue going out there every day. It's a win-win I'd say.' She chuckled, sipped her coffee, then glanced at her phone. 'I'd best be off, Harriet will be in by now and I want to see if she had any luck with Drum, about using his homestead for the new business.'

They walked out together, and Meggie's steps felt light. Being with Max, getting coffee then walking to their offices seemed right. Something a couple living together would do. She almost skipped after she left him at the door of the clinic. He brushed her lips with his and said quietly, 'Enjoy your day, Meggie.'

The door to her building was unlocked, and Ben Evans waved from his desk, his phone to his ear. She waved as she went by, turning the light on in her own office and dumping her handbag, before walking into Harriet's next door. She wasn't there. But Meggie knew Drum and Billie had returned from their trip the day before, maybe she was spending extra time with Drum, after they put Billie on the bus.

Meggie spent the morning speaking to local florists and her favourite baker, about working on the concept. The three photographers she called were all keen. One even said she'd been trying to get permission to take photos at Barrington Homestead for years but could never get old Charlie Gordon, Rose's grandfather, to agree. The photographer offered an excellent rate and Meggie booked her for the first elopement.

As she put her phone down, Meggie heard movement from the next office. Harriet must be in. The smile on her face froze when she stepped into Harriet's office. Her friend was red-eyed and pale.

'Harri! You don't look well!' Harriet sniffled, wiped one eye with a tissue. She waved an arm at Meggie, indicating for her to close the door. She did, then sat in the chair across from Harriet's desk.

Meggie looked at Harriet for a moment, but she didn't speak. Just wiped her eyes again. 'Has something happened with Drum, Harri? If he's not keen on the business idea, the photos at the homestead, it's not a problem.' Meggie hoped her business concept hadn't caused a rupture in her friends' relationship.

Harriet shook her head, then gave Meggie a watery smile. 'No, actually, that's the good news. He's happy to proceed, with some reservations about how often, how long and how much of the homestead we use. But all manageable.'

Meggie clapped her hands. 'Oh! Fabulous! Please thank him.' Pausing, she frowned, and leaned forward, reaching a hand across the desk to pat Harriet's for a moment. 'Then what is it Harri?'

Harriet sniffed, then pulled another tissue from the box on her desk and blew her nose. She shook her head sadly. 'Oh Meggie, it's just me. I'm not feeling well. I was fine last night, even slept over at Drum's most of the night. But just before dawn I woke up, the pain was bad.' She was clutching her stomach. 'Really bad. So, I slipped out of bed and nipped back to my cottage. I haven't told Drum. But Meggie, it's been so bad I could barely stand. It's taken me all morning just to get ready for work and come in.'

Meggie immediately stood, reaching her hand toward Harriet. 'You shouldn't be here Harri! Gosh! Let me take you to the doctor. Or the hospital. It could be your appendix, or maybe gall bladder. I don't know, but Harriet, we need to get you some help.'

'Ssh. Sit down Meggie.' Harriet frowned, waving Meggie back to her chair. 'I know what it is and there's nothing anyone can do.' She began crying again, her shoulders shaking, and Meggie walked around the desk, rubbing her friend's back until her sobs subsided. Harriet blew her nose again, then indicated Meggie should return to her chair.

Harriet sighed deeply. 'I've never told you about my injury.' Meggie shook her head. 'I was stabbed a couple of years ago, here, on this side.' She patted the right side of her lower abdomen. 'It was my own fault, tried to wrestle my handbag from a bag snatcher while getting on a train in Sydney.'

Meggie nodded, murmuring 'how awful' and 'I'm so sorry'.

Harriet continued. 'I have a lot of scar tissue on this side, from numerous surgeries. I was only just beginning to heal when I arrived in Barrington.' She looked up then. 'Drum knows, of course. You know. The scars. And I told Rose and Debbie a long time ago. I've never thought to mention it to you Meggie. I've healed. On the outside at least.' Her chin wobbled, but she took a breath and continued. 'I lost my tube, and ovary on this side. There were other internal injuries too. The doctors said I couldn't have children, too much scarring.' Her face rigid with grief, she blurted the next words out in a rush. 'It's what holds me back. With Drum. Knowing I can't have children. He says he doesn't care, he has Billie.' She trailed off, shaking her head. 'Anyway, there was always a chance I'd have internal problems. It's quite likely endometriosis. Or complications from the original injury. I'm terrified of further surgery Meggie. I just can't do it.' She laid her head on her arms and sobbed again. Meggie heard the door crack open and turned to see Ben Evans there, looking concerned. Meggie waved him away, mouthed *I've got this,* and he quietly closed the door.

Meggie admired Harriet. For her business acumen, her independence. She'd never seen a hint of vulnerability. But now, with her heart breaking for her friend, she was pleased Harriet could share this with her. Knowing this about Harriet just made her feel closer.

Harriet straightened, her face tear-streaked. She gave a wobbly smile, shaking her head. 'I'm sorry Meggie, to burden you with this. But I'm not ready to talk to Drum about it.'

Taking a deep breath, Meggie spoke firmly. 'Harri, you speak as if you know what's causing the pain. But really, you don't. It could be a number of things.' She tried to get a laugh from her friend. 'Maybe it *is* your appendix.' Her effort was rewarded by a half smile from Harriet. 'I know you don't want further surgery, but Harriet, you need to know what it is. Really. Complications from your old injury, or something else. And I agree, until you know what you're dealing with, maybe not telling anyone else is a good idea. But Harriet, you've told me. So, I'm involved now. And I'm your friend. We need a plan.' Meggie reached across the desk, picking up a notepad and pen.

'Firstly. Should we make an appointment to see your surgeon, or the main doctor who looked after you after the stabbing? I'm assuming that will be in Sydney?' Harriet nodded. Meggie continued. 'Or we can see someone more local, Taree perhaps, and have your files sent to them. We get a referral from Sydney or see a local GP for that.'

'We?' Harriet spoke quietly, but with more of her usual confidence.

Meggie nodded, saying firmly. 'We. I'm involved now. You're not going through this alone. We'll make appointments and I'll take you. We can tell Drum, and anyone who asks, that we're doing business stuff. If we go together, no one will question it. Then, when we know what you're dealing with, and what treatment is needed, you can share with Drum and those close to you.' Meggie added fiercely. 'Those who love you Harriet Russell.'

Harriet laughed, for the first time. 'I've never seen this side of you, Meggie Hamilton. I'm a little bit scared.'

Meggie relaxed slightly. 'You should be. No getting out of this. And we need to start now. We have to help you with the pain, and the sooner you find the cause, and treatment, the better. How do you want to proceed?'

Meggie saw Harriet's hand tremble as she picked up her

phone. 'I'll call the Sydney doctor, ask for a referral. But if he thinks I need to go to Sydney to see him ...'

'Sydney is no problem Harri. I'm still taking you, wherever you need to go.'

Harriet found the number and called.

14

S tepping into the clinic, he stopped for a moment to speak to Mrs Tubbs sitting straight-backed with her elderly cat, Ginger, on her lap. Almost blind, his whiskers were white and his coat a faded mustard colour. Max had told Mrs Tubbs last time that Ginger was struggling to eat, the teeth he had left were worn, and had recommended a change of diet, but he could see the old cat was thinner now.

It was just on opening time and as Melanie arrived through the back of the clinic, the front door opened and two customers walked in, both with dogs. After greeting them, he asked Mrs Tubbs and Ginger to come through.

'Take a seat Mrs Tubbs, I can examine Ginger while you hold him on your lap, he'll be more comfortable.' Max smiled in what he hoped was a reassuring manner.

'There's no need Max.' Mrs Tubbs looked up at him, her eyes filled with tears. 'He's in pain a lot of the time and has no interest in food. I hate seeing him this way.' She sniffed then and Max handed her a box of tissues. She took two and wiped her eyes with one hand, her other hand gently smoothing the fur on old Ginger's back.

Max sat beside Mrs Tubbs and took her hand in his. 'You're right Mrs Tubbs. He is struggling. We have something you can try, for the pain. One each morning in his food.' He waited. He guessed she'd already decided about the cat's future, but it was a difficult one and not to be rushed.

'He's on borrowed time as it is Max. He's almost eighteen, and up until the last six months, he's had a good life.' She shook her head sadly.

'You've provided the good life Mrs Tubbs.'

'It's time Max. Last time I came in I told you I wouldn't let him suffer. I know you've done all you can to help him and I'm grateful. But he is suffering.' She stood suddenly, almost thrusting the cat onto Max's lap. 'Please put him to sleep.' She walked to the door and spoke again but didn't look back. 'I've said my goodbyes, but I can't stay while you, while you ...' She left the room, closing the door firmly. Max stood, still holding the cat and walked through to the animal hospital section, placing Ginger in a comfortable cage.

Melanie popped her head around the door. 'Mrs Tubbs left without Ginger?'

'Yes, poor love. She's very upset. I'll see the other patients now and will euthanise old Ginger later this morning. I'll call her after to let her know and see if she wants him back for burial at her place.' Max gave Ginger a pat and closed the enclosure door.

'It's hard for her. Mr Tubbs died a few years ago and she's on her own now, old Ginger was her only companion,' Melanie sighed. 'If you're ready I'll send the next one in Max.'

'Thanks Melanie.'

The morning was busy, Angus dropped in to help with a surgery. A cattle dog with a broken tail, from a tumble off the back of a quad bike, the tail had been run over. They had to amputate almost half the length.

'How about lunch at the café, Max? If the clinic has finished for the day, I could do with a hand at home, separating cows and calves. Wee Charlie is at day care so Rose will help too.' Angus spoke while washing his hands and arms at the large sink in the surgery.

'Lunch sounds good.' He glanced over at Ginger. 'I still need to deal with Ginger, but it can wait until after lunch, he's sleeping now. I should do it before we head to your place.'

They strolled down to the café, chatting about the afternoon's work. While waiting for their order, Meggie rushed in. Max waved her over, but she seemed flustered. He raised his eyebrows at Angus. They watched as she ordered, then joined them, almost flopping into a chair.

'Everything okay Meggs?' Angus touched his sister lightly on the arm.

She seemed to straighten. 'Oh. Yeah. Just business. You know.' Something in the way she spoke didn't quite ring true to Max, but he wouldn't ask here, now. She waved her arm toward the counter. 'Picking up a bit of lunch for Harri too.' She turned suddenly toward Max. 'Can you and Tommy come for dinner tonight? Stay over?'

'Of course.' Max tried to speak normally, but he could feel Angus watching him. 'Around six? Can I bring something?'

'No. Just come.' Meggie glanced at the counter, Debbie was holding a bag up. 'That's my order. Gotta go.' She stood and walked quickly to Debbie who handed her the bag. She almost ran out the door with it.

'Something I should know Max?' Angus asked quietly as Debbie brought their meals over.

Setting their burger in front of them, Debbie stood looking at them in turn, hands on hips. 'Is Meggie okay? She seemed flustered.'

'I was just asking Max the same thing.' Angus drawled, eyebrows raised.

'I'm as confused as you are mate. But she's asked me for dinner, so maybe she'll tell me then.' Internally Max was worrying. Has she changed her mind about them moving in? But if that was worrying Meggie it was a conversation they'd have in private.

'It could just be the new business. She's keen as mustard to get it set up.' Angus picked up his burger and gave Max a lop-sided grin. Max sensed that Angus thought it was about their relationship too. His unease was heightened but he grinned back at Angus and wrapped his hands around his own burger. He'd wait until tonight.

Debbie seemed satisfied, returning to the counter where a small line of customers had formed.

Back at the clinic, Melanie advised she'd rescheduled two patients for the next day and would handle any walk-ins until closing time at three.

'I'll deal with Ginger and call Mrs Tubbs, then come out to your place Angus.' Max walked through to the surgery while Angus left through the rear door.

He set up the surgery for the procedure, then walked into the hospital section to retrieve Ginger. The old cat was still asleep, exactly where he'd left him earlier. He opened the door and reached in, then hesitated for a moment. He gently lifted the cat out. He wasn't breathing. Ginger had died peacefully in his sleep after Mrs Tubbs had left that morning. A blessing, he thought.

'Hello Mrs Tubbs, it's Max Masters here.'

'Is it over?' Her voice was shaky.

His words were gentle. 'It is, Mrs Tubbs, but not by my hand. Ginger died peacefully in his sleep sometime after you left. You knew he was ready to go, and it seems he just fell asleep and didn't wake up.'

'Really?' He heard the hesitation in her voice, perhaps wondering if he was simply trying to be kind.

'Really. I have the surgery set up for the procedure, but when I collected him he had already passed.' He heard her take a breath. 'Would you like me to bring him back later today or would you like us to take care of his body from here?'

'Bring him home please Max, I'd like to lay him to rest under the lemon tree, it was one of his favourite spots.'

'Alright Mrs Tubbs, I'll be there around five this afternoon.'

'Thank you.'

15

'Sydney tomorrow. They want to see me straight away.' Harriet nibbled her bottom lip. 'They're not surprised. They were expecting complications.' She shook her head.

'Okay, Sydney tomorrow. What time is your appointment? Should we leave today?' Meggie hoped her voice sounded bright and positive. Harriet was pale, but she'd said the pain had eased a bit.

'We need to be at his rooms at Royal North Shore Hospital at eleven. Honestly, if you don't mind an early start, I'd rather go in the morning.' Meggie was silently relieved. She'd invited Max and Tommy for dinner, wanted to give Max the keys to the apartment, in case she needed to be away the whole week.

'Morning is good.'

Harriet pushed the sandwich further away. She'd barely taken two bites. 'Surgeon first, then Gynaecologist if required. If it looks like Endometriosis.' Tears fell silently down her cheeks and Meggie pushed the tissue pack closer to her friend, her heart breaking. 'I've been reading, they'll probably recommend a hysterectomy. Straight away.'

'Harriet.' Meggie spoke firmly. 'You don't really know. Just wait until tomorrow, or the next day, depending how quickly they can make other appointments.'

Harriet wiped her eyes. 'I'm sorry Meggie. Thank you for being here. For coming tomorrow. I just don't think I could go through this with Drum right now. The uncertainty. And Billie. I don't want to upset Billie.' She looked away, then back at Meggie. 'But a hysterectomy is one of the better options. It could be cancer. I may need further bowel removal.' She sobbed again, shaking her head sadly. 'One bad decision, in a split second. And my life was changed forever.'

'Yes it was Harriet. But it's not all bad and you need to remember that.' Meggie's tone was firm now. Harriet's expression changed to one of shock. 'Yes, you had a terrible injury, a shocking experience. All the surgeries, the pain, the after affects. I can't begin to imagine.' She saw Harriet nod slightly at these words. 'But would you have found Barrington if you hadn't been through all this? Would you be with Drum and Billie, have your friendship with Debbie, Rose and Melanie? And me? Would we be starting a whole new business together?'

Harriet pushed her chair back roughly and strode around the desk, still crying. Meggie stood and Harriet was in front of her, trying to smile through her tears. 'You're right Meggie! Of course, you're right. I would never have come looking for a place to start over if I hadn't been stabbed that day. And I do love it here.' She threw her arms around Meggie, and she fiercely hugged her back.

'We're partners Harriet. And friends. And I'll see you

through this. Once you know what's causing the pain, and what treatment you need, you will tell your friends, those who love you. Including Drum. We'll all see you through this Harri.' Meggie patted her friend's back and said a silent prayer at the same time.

'I'll pick you up at six tomorrow, we can get breakfast on the way. I'll tell Ben that we're going to Sydney for a couple of days to sort supplies for the business, take some meetings.' She looked into Harriet's eyes. 'But you should consider telling Drum the truth tonight, Harriet.'

Shaking her head vigorously, Harriet's clenched her teeth. 'Not until I know. I want the facts. Just you Meggie, for now. Please.'

'Alright. Just me.'

'And no breakfast for me either. Make it six thirty and grab yourself something on the way. I'm nil-by-mouth from midnight in case they want to do an ultrasound or keyhole investigation.'

Meggie nodded. 'Alright. I'm going to do some work now. I might even check out some Sydney suppliers in case I have time to see them while I'm down there. Are you okay here? Should you go home and rest?'

'I'm going to do some work too. The pain isn't so bad. I need to finish a couple of things in case I'm away more than just two days. Oh, and we can stay at Drum's family apartment in the eastern suburbs, they're between tenants. Pack for a couple of days Meggie, but if I need to be there longer, well, we'll reassess. And I'll tell Drum.'

'Deal.'

TOMMY BURST INTO THE APARTMENT, SHE'D LEFT THE DOOR unlocked, and hugged her quickly. His hair was damp from the shower, and he was wearing clean jeans and jumper. 'Hi Meggie, how was your day?' She grinned back at his impish face. She was sure Max had told him to ask her that. Usually, his first question was *what's for dinner?*'

'My day was good. Very busy. You'll have to help me in the kitchen.' She leaned down just as Max walked in, closing the door behind him. She saw he had wine in his hand. 'We're having ravioli Bolognese and I need some cheese grated.'

'I'll do that! I know where everything is.' He flew across to the kitchen where she had everything set up on the bench. She turned to Max and whispered, 'Hello you.'

He pulled her close, kissed the tip of her nose, and replied. 'Hello you too. I have wine.'

'Good work, let's get that open and breathing.' She watched as Max did just that, then turned to check on Tommy. He'd grated more than enough cheese, so she helped him scrape it from the board into a bowl. 'Take that over to the table please Tommy. I have lemonade in the fridge, if you'd like a glass.'

'Yes please!' She stepped back as he helped himself, carefully pouring into a glass. She had to admit, Max had trained him well.

16

Max helped Meggie clean up while Tommy did his homework on the kitchen table. Max told her about Mrs Tubbs and Ginger, and how Tommy had gone to her house with him after school. They'd wrapped the old cat in the blanket Mrs Tubbs provided and Max had dug a grave beneath the lemon tree. Tommy had patted Mrs Tubbs hand after she threw the first handful of soil into the grave, then he distracted her with talk about Fred's puppies and how he'd fed his chickens after school.

'He's a good kid Max, and already sensitive to the grief of others. He'll make a very caring vet one day. Like his dad. And like my brother.' Meggie nudged Max with her shoulder, and they chuckled together.

'I'd ask you both to stay the night Max, but I invited you over for a reason, and that's not one of them.' She lowered her voice. 'Although I kinda wish it was, you smell good Max Masters.'

He grinned, happy to know she hadn't changed her mind. Good. But she did have something on her mind. He put the tea towel across the sink to dry and leaned back, arms folded, legs crossed at the ankles. He cocked an eyebrow. 'Better be a good reason then Meggie.' He watched her blush, then give him a cheeky look. His jeans felt tighter, and he straightened.

Meggie handed him a set of keys, placing them in his hand, she closed his fingers over them. 'Keys Max. It's just one set and you might want to make a front door key for Tommy too, and Indiana. Front and back door keys and another to the storage shed in the back yard. My suitcases are in there and a couple of boxes that Mum brought from home last time she was here.'

'Thank you. But why today? We're planning to move across on Saturday.' He was curious, and she seemed to have something on her mind, but he was sure now it wasn't cold feet.

'I'm going to Sydney tomorrow, early, with Harriet. You know, business supplies and some meetings etc.' Her eyes slid away from his, and he knew instinctively this wasn't the truth. Or not the whole truth anyway. He tensed. It wasn't like Meggie not to be open. Should he be worried?

He'd play it cool. See what else she said. 'Okay. Going for just a day or two, or do you think it will be the whole week, hence the keys?' He dangled the keys in his hand.

Meggie sighed then looked directly at him. 'Honestly Max. I'm going for Harriet. She has some things she needs help with, and I can do some business while I'm there. I'm hoping a couple of days, but it may be the rest of the week.' She was looking at him, but not really seeing him for a moment and he suddenly realised she was keeping a confidence for Harriet. He pulled her against him.

'Take as long as you need. And thank you for the keys.' She

nodded, the tension left her shoulders and she leaned against him, her breath against his neck. She whispered *thank you* and he knew that whatever was going on with Harriet was causing her concern. He wouldn't add to it. He wouldn't ask. He'd just be there. Be here, when Meggie got back.

'It's almost bedtime for Tommy. We'll go, let you get some sleep if you're leaving early tomorrow.' Max helped Tommy pack his books up, they said good night and walked to the door.

He watched Tommy turn back and hug Meggie, saying goodnight and thanking her for dinner. She hugged him back. His little face radiated happiness, and Max loved her even more. Her lips met his, then she murmured, 'I'll stay in touch Max, let you know when I'm coming home.'

'No pressure Meggie, but if you feel like a chat, at any time, I'll be here.'

THE NEXT COUPLE OF DAYS DRAGGED FOR MAX, THE HIGHLIGHT being their visits to Fred Saunders each day. He seemed to be holding his own and Max was sure he looked forward to their visits too. The five puppies were thriving. Tommy seemed to favour one, a male with a slightly wonky ear. Max was fond of the smallest one himself, a female.

Meggie had messaged, said she hoped to be home on Thursday. She hadn't offered an explanation and he hadn't asked.

He and Angus attended Drum Murray's property on Thursday after lunch, to vaccinate his weaners. They worked solidly for ninety minutes, then took a break. There was a cold wind blowing down from the tops, and the men huddled together by the yards drinking coffee from a thermos.

'Harri and Meggie are due back today.' Drum narrowed his eyes when he spoke, and Max wasn't sure about his tone.

He replied lightly. 'So I hear. They've been busy.'

Angus looked from one to the other. 'Am I missing something lads?' He turned to Drum. 'If you don't mind me saying, you seem tense mate.'

Drum tipped the last of his coffee onto the grass. His shoulders dropped. 'Angus. I just don't know. She said they had business meetings, but she's usually excited about that stuff. She's been quiet. She seemed unwell on Sunday but wouldn't tell me anything.'

His voice grew more strident as he turned to Max. 'Do you know anything? I feel like she's holding back from me and Billie. And she's been. I don't know. Sad. I asked if her parents are okay, and she said they're fine.' He stopped, turned away. Angus lay his hand on Drum's shoulder.

'Women mate. It may be nothing. Best not to speculate. If Max knew anything, he'd say.' Max blanched, and Angus saw him. He began packing up their stuff, mumbling something about getting moving or he'd be late picking Tommy up from school and their afternoon chores at Fred Saunders.

Drum turned back to Max. 'Do you know anything Max?' his face was anguished.

Max looked him in the eye. 'I don't Drum. Meggie gave me the same story about going to Sydney for business meetings. She didn't elaborate. I didn't ask.' He took a deep breath. 'But we're mates Drum, and I will say, I think there's more to the story too. But I trust that Meggie will tell me if it's something I need to know.'

He was relieved when Angus gave him a nod of approval. 'I'd be the same with Rose. But she only keeps information back if it's a surprise or she's got a problem but wants to wait until she has the solution before telling me.'

Drum agreed. 'Harriet is very independent. Maybe that's it. And if Meggie is in her confidence, perhaps it is a business thing. I just hope the solution doesn't involve her wanting to leave Barrington.'

'There hasn't been any mention of that Drum. Hopefully, you'll find out tonight.' Max suggested.

17

'We'll be in Barrington before dusk.' Meggie fiddled with the radio then turned it off. She glanced at Harriet, her friend had dark circles under her eyes but seemed more at peace than she had before the trip. At least she knows now, and in another week she'd have all the facts.

'Did I ever tell you how I met Drum the first time?' Harriet laughed and Meggie was thrilled to hear it.

'I don't think you did. Tell me.'

'It was just past here, after driving through Stroud, that I hit a kangaroo.' She looked at Meggie, grinning. 'In the Alfa. Drum was behind me, saw the 'roos with his higher lights before I did, and tried to warn me. I was just annoyed he was tailing me so closely, but it had made me slow right down.'

'Ouch. Poor Alfie. Were you injured?'

'I wasn't, but my old injury was still healing and at first I thought I'd opened it up. Drum yanked open the car door and tried to help me out but all I saw was this man-giant grabbing at me. I think I told him to back off.' She giggled and Meggie laughed too, she could just picture it. Harriet was feisty.

'Drum may have been more scared than you were.' She ventured a glance at Harriet, who threw her head back and laughed, really laughed, for the first time all week.

'Perhaps.' Harriet wiped her eyes. 'I had no idea, then, that we'd end up together.' They drove on in companionable silence, until Meggie slowed to drive through Barrington, heading to Harriet's little cottage.

'When are you going to tell Drum?' Meggie spoke quietly, then waited.

'At the end of next week. When I know for sure.' They were at the cottage now and Meggie stopped the engine. 'I'm sorry Meggs, for asking you to say nothing until then. But I appreciate everything you've done this week. All the appointments. It would have been hard on my own. I thought about calling Mum, asking her to come up, but I'm glad I didn't. I'll tell them when I know for sure too.'

Meggie reach across, taking Harriet's hand in hers. 'You know I'm going to pray for the best possible outcome Harri, but if it's the worst, I'm here for you.'

'I know Meggie. Thank you.'

IT WAS AFTER SIX WHEN MEGGIE PULLED UP BEHIND HER building. The light over the back stairs was on and she suspected Max and Tommy were there. He'd said not to worry about dinner. She wondered if he was planning to take her to the pub. She was tired, it had been a long drive and even longer week. All the highs and lows. She felt less like cooking, so the pub would have to do.

She grabbed her bag from the back seat and started toward the stairs. The door at the top opened and Max hurried down. 'Meggie.' He took her bag in one hand and wrapped his arm around her shoulders, kissing the top of her head. 'You're home.'

Meggie leaned into him, savouring his warmth and strength. 'Home.' She whispered.

Following him up the stairs, she could smell something delicious. At the top she raised her eyebrows. 'Have you cooked dinner, Max Masters.'

'Ha ha, hope you like it. Lamb shanks in the slow cooker. I put it on this morning, it's been simmering all day.' Meggie was surprised. He'd said he could cook, but she hadn't seen much evidence. But of course, he didn't really have the facilities in the tiny flat at the clinic.

'Love lamb shanks. Slow cooked or otherwise. Smells divine.'

Tommy appeared, a tea towel over his shoulder. 'Hi Meggie, welcome home.' He sidled close and she wrapped an arm around him. He smelled of soap, and faintly of garlic. He'd have helped, of course. 'I've set the table, and Dad?'

'Yes mate.'

'The meat is falling apart. We need to eat it. Now.' He almost pulled Max through to the kitchen.

Meggie took her bag from Max. 'Give me two minutes to freshen up Tommy. Serve it up, I'll be right there.'

From her room she could hear Tommy's happy chatter and Max's deeper responses. She really did feel like she was home.

Despite the week she'd had with Harriet, she wouldn't be anywhere else right now.

Hours later Tommy was asleep in the spare room. No in *his* room. And she and Max were sipping wine on the couch, her legs in his lap as he gently rubbed her feet.

'I could get used to this Max. Foot rubs in lieu of rent.' She laid her head back, sighing.

'Foot rubs plus rent Meggie. I take it you've had a hectic week?' She cracked open an eye.

'Yes. Hectic indeed.' She closed her eyes again.

'So, you did the business stuff?' All good?' He was prying. They both knew it.

'Some business stuff. All good.' She withdrew her feet, finished her wine in one gulp and stood up. 'I'm happy I'm home. Dinner was the best. I have one more demand before I fall asleep on my feet.'

'Anything Meggie. Anything at all.' Max surged to his feet.

Stepping into his arms she lay her head against his broad shoulder. 'Take me to bed and make love to me. Sweet gentle love.' His arms tightened, holding her firmly against him.

'There's nothing I'd rather do. I love you Meggie Hamilton.'

Forty-five minutes later Meggie whispered, 'And I love you Max Masters,' as she fell asleep in his arms.

18

Max felt like he was walking on air all day. They were officially moving in tomorrow and sleeping over tonight too. He'd had the best night with Meggie, had never felt so close to her. He knew, in his heart, that they were good together, that she was his future. They were going to the pub for dinner tonight with Melanie, Ben and young Tiffany.

He picked Tommy and Tiffany up after school, Tommy wanted to take her to see the puppies at Fred Saunders' place. Fred was on the veranda, as usual, when they pulled up. His daughter Sally's car was still there. Sometimes she stayed over and other times she went home. Stepping out of the car Tommy waved to Fred, who smiled and waved back. Taking Tiffany by the hand they ran around the side of the house. Max had impressed upon Tommy that he must do his chores, lock the chickens in and feed them, not just play with the puppies.

'Good afternoon Fred. How's the day treating you?' Max stepped onto the veranda and sat down beside Fred.

'Good, Max. Sally's been here cooking and cleaning. I could eat off that floor.' He laughed, then held his handkerchief to his mouth with a shaky hand. There was blood on the cloth. They both saw it. Fred continued, speaking more slowly. 'It's getting closer Max, I can feel it creeping up on me.' He snorted then. 'But I take comfort in the cleanliness of my floors.' Sally stepped out, smiled at Max as her father spoke. 'If I fall down getting one of Sally's casseroles out of the oven when I'm alone, I can just eat it right there where I fall.' His words surprised Max so much that he let out a hearty laugh.

'I think you're still okay Fred, if you make off-colour jokes like that.' He saw Fred still had a twinkle in his eye and Sally retreated inside, saying 'stop it Dad', as she went.

Fred leaned back. 'I won't die on her shift. Max, I'd rather you find me. Not Tommy though, you need to protect Tommy from seeing me like that.'

Surprised again, Max looked closely at Fred. His eyes were watery, his hands shaky. He'd lost more weight in the last couple of weeks, and he realised what an effort he was making with Sally there. 'You don't need to make an effort for me Fred. I want you to know that you can call me, day or night, if you feel poorly.' And stressed the point with a look.

Sally stepped out again. 'I'm going to check the puppies before I go Dad.' She turned to Max. 'My brother will be here in the morning and Dad seems well today.' Fred murmured something and watched as she walked around the house, taking the path the children had taken shortly before.

'I'm not poorly Max. I'm dying. I can feel it.' He shook his head. 'My beautiful girl, she wants so badly to believe I'm doing better.'

'We all want that Fred.' Max sat quietly with the old man, his heart breaking for him, but needing to be stoic. Sally returned, chatted with them for a moment, then kissed her father goodbye and left.

Max stood. 'I'll go around back and check on the kids.' He strode around the house, his own emotions barely in check. The chickens were fed and locked in, and the puppies were feeding from their mum, but Tommy and Tiffany were nowhere in sight.

'Tommy!' Max called, not too loudly. Tommy popped his head out of the shed where the animal feed was kept.

'Kittens, Dad.' He disappeared. Max strolled over. Poking his head in the door, he waited for his eyes to adjust to the gloom.

'Over here, Dad.' Leaving the door open, he stepped inside, making his way to where Tommy and Tiffany sat on a bale of hay, three kittens playing between them.

'How old do you think they are Dad? I can't see their mum around.'

Max took the one Tommy held out. He gave it a pat and it purred, loudly for something so small. The children laughed. 'Six or seven weeks old, I'd say. Big enough to leave their mother but not really old enough to fend for themselves without her.'

He picked each one up in turn. Two females and a male. They needed vaccinating and worming. They didn't look feral. The male was bright orange and white, the other two were mottled, their fur a darker brown. He picked up the male again, holding it out to Tommy. 'Does this one remind you of anything?'

'Ginger. Mrs Tubbs old cat that died.' Tommy's certainty was pleasing.

'Mrs Tubbs lives on the other side of town, so it can't be related. But it does look a lot like him.' Max agreed. 'Come on kids, we'd better go. We need to clean up for our dinner at the pub tonight.' The kids set the kittens down and Tiffany was already outside when Max had a thought. 'Tommy, wait a moment. Bring the ginger one with you.'

Max watched Tommy scoop it up and carrying it against his body he followed Tiffany back to the house.

'There's chocolate slice inside, Sally left some on a plate for you.' Fred waved the children inside. Tommy handed the kitten to Max and dashed inside after Tiffany, yelling, 'We have to wash our hands first Tiff!'

He handed the kitten to Fred. 'What's this Max?'

'The kids found three of them in the feed shed. Two females and this little bloke.' Max watched as Fred held the kitten up, turned it around, looked at it closely.

'Not a bad looking cat. Descended from one my old dad had here when we first got married. We don't feed them, they've always lived in the sheds, keep the mice down. I didn't realise there was a new litter.' Fred handed it back to Max.

'Fred, do you know Mrs Tubbs? Elaine Tubbs?'

'Elaine. Of course. I was mates with her husband George. He passed away a few years ago. Haven't seen her in a while. Neither of us drives. Why?'

'She had a big old ginger cat. Eighteen years old. He died this week.' Max held the kitten up. 'This one has the same colouring.'

'Ha! George hated that cat, but Elaine doted on him. He was from one of our litters, years ago. George needed a ratter, but Elaine turned him into a house-cat and George came out and got another one for his shed. Never told Elaine.' Fred grinned and Max chuckled. 'But I can see why you're asking. You think Elaine might like the kitten?'

Max nodded. 'I do. We buried the old cat for her, under her lemon tree, earlier this week.'

'She can have it, I've no use for it. Happy to see it go. It won't be a worker though; she'll make it a house-cat too.' Max chuckled at Fred's obvious dislike of house cats.

'I'll take it then. I'll drop it into the clinic, worm and vaccinate it and take it to Elaine tomorrow. If she doesn't want it, I'm sure I can find a home for it.' Max walked to the front door, peering inside. 'That's enough Tommy, one piece only. We're going to the pub remember.'

Back outside he grinned at Fred. 'Pretty sure he's already had two pieces.'

'Good. My kids will think I'm eating better.' Fred coughed again but still managed a small smile.

With the kids in the back of the car, the kitten on an old blanket between them, Max waved to Fred as he backed out. He watched as his old friend shuffled inside. When the door closed, he turned the car and drove out, listening to the kids' happy chatter.

19

Dinner at the pub was a welcome distraction and Meggie enjoyed the conversation, especially when Max began quizzing Ben on the local property market. She knew prices had increased during the covid years and Ben explained that most were selling before they were officially listed, as he had a network of interested buyers just waiting for the right opportunities.

Max seemed a bit deflated by this, but talked through what he was looking for with Ben, and included Meggie in the conversation, making it obvious they were looking for a home together in the future. Despite hearing from Ben that currently there wasn't much around that met their needs, Meggie was warmed by the knowledge that Max had no doubts at all about their future.

Melanie had brought a card game and Tiffany and Tommy were playing at one end of the table, their dinners finished.

'Clever mama,' Meggie murmured to Mel, who chuckled. 'Years of practice. I was a single mum for a long time, Tiff came everywhere with me. I was lucky with work, first Doctor Petersen, then Angus when he bought the practice. I've always been able to work school hours and have her with me in school holidays on days she wasn't with friends or my mother.' Mel inclined her chin towards Ben and Max, now deep in conversation about working cattle dogs. 'Ben has been great; a huge support and Tiff adores him.' She hesitated, lowered her voice. 'We've spoken recently about, um, having one together.' She blushed, and Meggie thought Melanie had never looked lovelier.

Leaning in, Meggie almost whispered. 'Spoken about? Or already, um, manufacturing?' She giggled, eyebrows raised, as she realised Melanie hadn't taken more than a sip of the wine in front of her while Meggie was on her second glass.

Melanie's face closed over for a brief moment. Meggie reached across, touching her hand. 'I'm joking Mel, you don't have to answer that.' Although her expression already confirmed Meggie's assumption.

'Wait. Just a second.' Melanie tapped Ben on the arm. He turned immediately, his face full of concern. And love. Meggie almost held her breath as he moved closer to his wife. 'Everything okay Mel?' She nodded happily, then gestured for Max to come closer too.

With a quick glance at the children, still absorbed in their game, she said, 'Actually, Ben and I were going to tell you tonight, if we found the right moment.'

Ben put his arm around Melanie and looked from Max to Meggie, beaming. 'We're expecting.'

Meggie reached across, hugging Melanie while Max pumped Ben's hand. 'Well done mate, great news.' He leaned across, kissed Melanie on the cheek. 'Happy for you both. Yes, really happy.'

'Happy about what Dad?' Tommy slid closer to his father, his young face full of curiosity. Tiffany looked closely at her mother, who nodded. The little girl turned to her friend and said in a very matter-of-fact tone, 'Mummy's having a baby. I'm getting a little sister.'

'Or brother.' Ben chimed in. 'We don't know yet Tiff.'

'Sister. It's a girl. I want a sister.' Tiffany was firm and the adults laughed when Tommy said, 'Oh, is that all. I thought you were getting a pony, or something good.' He slid back to where the cards lay on the table and Tiffany joined him.

Meggie snorted. Max sighed, his eyes raised toward the ceiling for a moment. 'Priorities in the world of Tommy Masters.'

Melanie spoke again. 'We only told Tiff this afternoon, because we wanted to tell you tonight. She was excited for about five minutes and now just accepts it.' She made a face. 'That's good isn't it? She's been an only child ...'

Meggie was about to speak, to reassure her, but Max was quicker. 'Indi was only a couple of years younger than Tiff when Liliana fell pregnant with Tommy. She took it in her stride, and you've seen them together. They're really close.' He winked at Meggie. 'As close as you'd expect anyway. It's great news. Um, does Angus know yet?'

'No. We're dropping out to the homestead tomorrow morning. We'll tell him and Rose then. But Max, I'm feeling great, haven't had much morning sickness and I'm twelve weeks now, so I expect to keep working ...' She trailed off.

'Melanie, you know we'll work around you. You can work as much, or as little, as you need to. I just don't want to let it slip to Angus until you've had a chance to tell him.' He reached over and gave her hand a reassuring pat. 'You've got us so organised at the clinic, you could probably run it remotely.' They laughed and Meggie was gratified to hear Max's only concern was for Melanie's well-being.

'There's ice-cream for dessert Dad, on the kid's menu.' Tommy was back, nudging his father. Tiffany nodded, her blonde ponytail bouncing up and down as she did.

'Kids' dessert then.' Max looked at the others. 'How about the adults? I'm keen on the apple strudel.'

'I'll share that with you Max.' Meggie grinned at him. They rarely had dessert at the pub, but when they did, they shared.

Ben piped up. 'I'm partial to the sticky date pudding.' He glanced at Melanie, then whispered, 'Melanie. Doesn't. Share.' Melanie dug him in the ribs, but laughingly agreed. 'He's right. I'm into dessert right now. Cheesecake for me please Max.'

Meggie leaned back as Max and Ben went to order dessert while Melanie slipped off to the bathroom. Tommy and Tiffany were still playing their game, although she'd seen Tiffany yawn more than once. She looked around the pub, almost full, typical Friday night. Two men at the bar, farmers who looked familiar, were chatting with Ben and Max and a couple of people had smiled at Meggie, greeting her when she arrived. Something shifted inside her, she let out a breath, thinking about it for a moment. Tears sprang to her eyes. Contentment. Security. Happiness. She'd found her place, here in this little town. Her place and her tribe and it was a feeling she couldn't quite describe. Her eyes roved back to the bar. Max was looking at her, Ben was still in conversation. She placed her hand on her heart and smiled, hoping her expression matched the depth of her feeling, in that moment. He spoke briefly with Ben, then strode back to her. 'I saw that look Meggie Hamilton.' He kissed her quickly and as the others returned, held her hand in his, beneath the table.

20

Moving in with Meggie didn't take long and Tommy spent over an hour in his new room, putting away a selection of books, games and puzzles that had never been unpacked in the flat.

Max added some books of his own to the shelves in the living area. Meggie placing them on the shelf as he unpacked a box. She held one up. 'John Grisham fan?'

Max laughed. 'You bet. And James Patterson, Lee Child and Chris Hammer, he's an Aussie author. I like crime and mystery, mostly, but don't mind something with a bit of history in it too.' He handed her the last two books, then ran his fingers along the spines of Meggie's books. 'A lot of women authors here. Romance?'

Meggie snorted and rolled her eyes. 'Women authors yes. Mostly Australian. Some indie.'

'Indie?'

'Independent authors.' He watched her pull three books

from the shelf. 'You'd like these. Rhonda Forrest, Queensland author. This trilogy starts in the depression years and moves through World War Two and beyond. Our lads in New Guinea.' She pointed to other books. 'All Aussies, all women. Crime, mystery, small town. Oh, this one, dual timeline. Loved it.'

He pulled her into his lap, sitting beside the bookshelf. 'I'm picturing us now. Sipping port in the evenings and reading companionably. I'll read some of yours if you read some of mine.'

'We could. Do that. In the evenings.' She giggled and wriggled around in his lap, winding her arms around his neck, reaching up to place her lips on his. 'You know. When we have nothing better to do.' He hardened immediately but was conscious of Tommy only a room away.

'Minx.' He was about to say more, but Tommy, as if sensing his thoughts, appeared in the doorway.

'Is it time for morning tea yet Dad? I'm hungry.' He grinned, his head cocked to one side. 'What are you two doing?'

Meggie quickly jumped up, her face flushed. She ran a hand through her thick hair, lifting it from her forehead. 'Morning tea sounds great. Have you ever made scones?'

'No. But I do love scones.' Tommy was eager, already trotting to the kitchen.

Meggie followed him for a few steps, then turned, winking at Max. 'You might want to take those empty boxes down to the storage shed while we start the scones.' He made a face but laughed to himself as she continued to the kitchen. Standing, he adjusted his jeans, folded the box flat and went in search of empty boxes in Tommy's room. He loved Meggie's playfulness. He had a lifetime of it to look forward to.

~

MAX AND TOMMY CHECKED ON THE LITTLE GINGER KITTEN, worming and vaccinating it. They drove out to Mrs Tubbs' house on the eastern side of town. Tommy was excited about gifting the kitten and held it inside his jumper, where it purred loudly. Max hoped it wasn't too soon, and that Mrs Tubbs would accept it.

She opened the door straight away, pleased to see them. 'Hello Max, and young Tommy. Your timing is good, I've just baked some cookies, they're still warm from the oven.'

Tommy opened his mouth to speak, but Max nudged him. He didn't want to tell her they'd just eaten two scones each. 'Thank you, that's lovely. I can smell them from here.' He turned to Tommy. 'Take your boots off Tommy.' Max followed her inside, Tommy appearing a minute later, the kitten still inside his jumper.

They sat at her kitchen table while she bustled around with plates and made a pot of tea. Tommy was bursting to tell her, so Max gave him a nod, grinning.

'I 'spose you're wondering why we're here, Mrs Tubbs?' Tommy's voice was higher than usual, his excitement obvious. She smiled, knowing something was up, but Max was sure she hadn't guessed.

'I was wondering just that, young Tommy. But I think you're about to tell me.' She placed a cookie on a plate and pushed it across the table to Tommy. He began to stand, his hand on his chest where the kitten wriggled.

Mrs Tubbs drew in a sharp breath. 'What have you got Tommy? It better not be a frog!' She looked at Max and began to stand. Max reached over, touched her arm and shook his head. 'It's not a frog.'

Tommy pulled the kitten from the bottom of his jumper as he walked around the table, placing it in Mrs Tubbs lap. 'It's a little ginger one, Mrs Tubbs. It needs a new home.'

Max watched as she tentatively placed her hand on the little creature. It immediately curled up, purring loudly. 'Well, I'll be. It's the dead spit of old Ginger!' She looked at it wonderingly, her hand gently patting its tiny body. Looking up, her eyes roved from Max to Tommy and back to Max. 'Wherever did it come from?'

Tommy jumped in quickly. 'From Mr Saunders' place. I've been helping with his animals after school and found the kittens on Friday. There were three of them. This one is a boy and the other two aren't ginger.' He slid back into his chair, picked up a biscuit and took a big bite. 'Mmm. Nice. Thank you.' He mumbled.

'Fred said your old Ginger was from his place too.' Max tickled the little cat behind the ears. 'He's been wormed and vaccinated.' He stopped. He wasn't sure if she knew Fred was ill.

She spoke quietly. 'How is Fred? I've been meaning to give him a call.'

He glanced at Tommy, who was reaching for a second biscuit. 'He's not well. But his family is there every weekend, and we've been helping with his animals. He has no use for the kitten. You'll be doing him a favour if you keep it.'

Mrs Tubbs beamed, at the same time nodding her understanding of Fred's situation. 'Of course I'll keep him. And I'll give Fred a call to thank him.' She turned to Tommy. 'What shall I call him Tommy?'

'I reckon you should call him Ginge. Not Ginger, that's a big cat's name. He's still so little. Just Ginge.' Tommy spoke with certainty and Max tried not to laugh.

'Ginge he is then.' Max stood as she spoke, indicating to Tommy they were leaving. 'Wait Max, take some biscuits home with you. With the kitten in one hand, she found an old-fashioned biscuit tin and tipped the whole plate of biscuits in, before closing the lid and passing it to Tommy. 'Thank you Max. And Tommy. For thinking of me.' She hugged the little cat to her chest. 'And you have a new patient now. Ginge Tubbs.'

Back in the car, Tommy grinned at Max. 'That was good, wasn't it Dad?'

Max reached across, poked Tommy in the ribs, making him laugh. 'It was really good Tommy.'

THE REST OF THE WEEKEND PASSED QUICKLY. HE'D TAKEN TOMMY to a rugby game at the local oval, then on an emergency call to a sheep farm to conduct an autopsy. He'd been impressed by Tommy's interest. He wasn't squeamish at all when Max opened the belly of the sheep, finding a large ball of hay twine in its abdomen. While the farmer didn't like losing an animal, he was relieved it wasn't poisoning which had been his first assumption. Finding the plant or weed causing it on a large property would have been problematic.

They drove out to Fred Saunders' place on Sunday afternoon but saw Jake's car there, so decided not to go in. Jake would check the animals.

On Sunday night, after dinner and a movie at home, Max took a shower before bed. Tommy was already asleep in his room. He heard Meggie on the phone as he stepped out of the shower. She sounded tense.

Walking into the bedroom, wearing pyjama bottoms and tee shirt, he saw Meggie sitting on the bed, the phone still in her hand, shoulders slumped. Walking to her side, he placed a hand gently on her shoulder. 'What is it Meggs? Can I help?'

She looked up at him, tears in her eyes, but shook her head. 'Harri. It's Harri. She's been a bit.' She stopped and drew in a deep breath.

He waited. 'A bit?' He asked softly.

Meggie shook her head. 'Just a bit. Down. Wanted a quick chat.' Her face was anguished as she looked up at him. 'I can't tell you Max. I wish I could. She's dealing with something and I'm supporting her as much as I can.' A tear slid down her cheek. 'I worry for her.'

Sitting on the bed beside her, Max pulled her into his arms. 'You're a good friend Meggie. And I'm sure Harriet would do the same for you. You don't have to tell me anything, but you can lean on me. Always.' He felt her shudder and held her firmly, one hand rubbing her back.

She buried her face in his neck, shuddered again, then sobbed. 'Oh Max. It's been awful, this last week.' She cried, great gulping sobs.

He held her murmuring, 'It's okay, let it out.' Until finally, she quietened, the tension leaving her shoulders as she collapsed into him. They sat like that for a while, until she straightened her shoulders and leaned back. He rubbed the tears beneath her eyes with the pad of his thumb and she lay her cheek against his hand.

'I'm sorry Max. I'm not usually so emotional. But she's my friend.' She gulped, pulled a tissue from the box beside the bed and blew her nose noisily. 'And you've only just moved in. I'm sorry.'

'Don't be sorry. We're in a relationship Meggie. I'm here for you. Living together changes the dynamic. It won't always be sexy fun and games. Real life isn't like that.' He watched her process this, nodding as he spoke. He squeezed her again. 'Can I get you anything? There's water beside the bed for you.'

She shook her head, then stood. 'Thank you. You know, I've never really lived with anyone before. Well, not a boyfriend anyway.' She was smiling now, tentatively.

'Boyfriend. Hmmm. I'm a bit old to be a boyfriend.' He laughed quietly.

'Partner?' She was grinning now, some of her cheekiness reappearing.

'Nah. Don't like partner much. Sounds like a business venture.' He waited.

'Lover?' She frowned after she asked. 'That sounds a bit racy. You know, we have Tommy to think of.'

He had something in mind. It had been on his mind since her brother's wedding. But he didn't want to bring it up now while she was upset about Harriet.

'Bloke?' He watched her face light up as she said it. 'Yep. That's a keeper. You're my bloke.' She threw herself against him, pushing him flat on the bed, sprawling on top of him.

'Bloke works for me. Missy.' He rolled her over, straddling her body, looking down at her face, still damp with tears, but so beautiful.

'Missy? I can live with that.' She pulled him down, his chest pressed hard on hers. 'What did you say about sexy fun and games. I've forgotten.'

He kissed her.

THE WEEK FLEW BY, EXCEPT MAX FOUND IT A STRUGGLE TO LEAVE the bed he shared with Meggie to go to Fred Saunders' place with Tommy before work. Tommy had begun to leap onto their bed in the mornings to 'wake them up.' After the first time Max noticed Meggie always had her pyjamas on before he came in. But she had to retrieve them from the floor beside the bed where they'd been tossed earlier in the evening. And she left a breakfast bowl and cereal on the kitchen counter before she went to bed, so they could tell him to have breakfast while they dressed. Showered and dressed usually. Sometimes together. Tommy didn't seem to care. He hovered in the kitchen each morning before they left, saying 'have a great day' to Meggie, his little face lighting up when she responded with a hug and a kiss to the top of his head.

She continued to worry about Harriet, but on Thursday night she told him they'd been invited to Drum's for a barbecue dinner on Saturday. Melanie and Ben, Angus and Rose, Debbie and Jamie, themselves and all the assorted children. With Drum and Harriet hosting the barbecue, surely that signalled their relationship was okay. Max hoped it meant good news, but Meggie still seemed worried.

ON FRIDAY MORNING FRED SAUNDERS WAS SITTING IN HIS USUAL place on his front veranda and Max caught his breath as he drove in. Something about Fred's stance didn't look right, but perhaps he was asleep. He sent Tommy straight around to feed the chickens and dogs and walked up the steps, speaking quietly to Fred as he did. If the old man was asleep, he didn't want to startle him.

Fred didn't respond, or stir at all, and Max placed his fingers over his thin wrist. His body was cold, and Max said a silent prayer for his old friend. He had died at home, on his farm, as he'd wanted. Thinking suddenly of Tommy, Max walked back into the garden and called Fred's daughter Sally, then the local police and ambulance. Sally thanked him through her tears and said she'd contact the rest of the family.

Tommy rounded the corner at full pelt, telling Max about the puppies' antics and that the chickens were fed and let out. He looked around, asked if Fred was asleep, before climbing into the car. Max simply nodded and left it at that. He'd tell Tommy the truth after school.

21

S uch a shame one of the best weeks of her life had been tempered by sadness, Meggie thought as she closed the office on Friday. Harriet had barely been in this week, and although Meggie knew it was important she rest while awaiting confirmation of her final test results, but she missed her energy. More than once Meggie had walked to Harriet's office to share some news or brainstorm an idea, only to realise she wasn't there. And while Harriet said she could call anytime; Meggie hadn't wanted to disturb her. Yet the invitation to the barbecue tomorrow night was heartening, as Harriet had said she would share her news with her closest friends.

Then, only this morning Max had dropped into her office just after she opened, telling her about finding Fred Saunders, who passed away while sitting on his veranda looking out over his paddocks. Max was distressed about keeping the news from Tommy, but Meggie agreed it was better to wait until the end of the day to explain, when they would all be together.

She sighed. This time last week they'd been heading to the pub for dinner with Mel and Ben and looking forward to Max and Tommy moving in. Stepping into the apartment, she felt the presence of Max and Tommy, although neither could be seen. She set her handbag down, and walked to the fridge, thinking to open a bottle of wine. Maybe they'd just get some takeaway tonight, she didn't feel like cooking.

Opening the fridge she saw three pizzas, already made but not yet cooked, stacked on one shelf. She could have cried. Max. Thoughtful man. She turned, and there he was, walking toward her, arms open. She snuggled against him, while he murmured, 'how was your day?'

Stepping back, she looked at him closely. 'More to the point, how was your day after I saw you this morning? And how is Tommy?' She looked over his shoulder for a moment. 'Where is Tommy?'

'He's good, having a shower. I picked him up from school at lunchtime after Mel said that word had got around about Fred. I didn't want him to hear about it from anyone else.' He took the wine from her hands and opened the bottle as he spoke, pouring two glasses. 'He went quiet when I told him, but said he already knew Fred was very sick. He thought it was nice he had died in his sleep, sitting on the veranda of his house.' Max handed a glass to Meggie and walked toward the sofa. She followed him. 'His main concern was to ask who would look after the puppies and chickens and I told him that Sally had already asked if we could keep doing that for a week or two while the family sorted out the funeral, then the property.'

'Did Sally say what they'd do with Fred's place, you know, after?' Meggie was trying to get a picture of it in her mind. She'd seen it from the road but had never been to the house.

'I think one of the grandsons is keen to keep it. But Sally said it might take a while to sort everything out. She offered to pay us to keep looking after the animals. Of course, I said no. I wanted to mention that Fred had promised a puppy for Tommy, but it didn't seem the right time to bring it up.' Max leaned his head back against the sofa. 'And Tommy has never known about the agreement, so if it doesn't happen, it's okay.'

'No. Not the right time to discuss. After the funeral you might be able to have a conversation.' Meggie was about to say more but Tommy appeared, already in pyjamas, hair damp from the shower. She set her glass down and made room for him between her and Max on the sofa.

He hesitated for a moment. 'I came home from school early and helped Dad at the clinic. Then we made pizzas for dinner.' He gave his father a questioning look.

'Meggie knows about Fred, son.' Meggie put her arms around him, and he cried, big gulping sobs. Tommy's chin wobbled, then he threw himself between them. They didn't speak, just waited until his sobs turned to sniffles. He sat up and Meggie handed him a tissue.

'Blow.' She watched as he took the tissue and blew his nose noisily. He handed the tissue to his father, who told him to just drop it on the floor for the moment.

'It's sad when someone dies Tommy, but you know Fred had a good long life.' Meggie spoke gently.

'I know Meggie. I'm sad about Fred, he was really lovely and trusted me to look after his animals.' Tommy said this with a hint of pride.

'Yes, he did trust you with his animals Tommy.'

Tommy wiped his eyes with the back of his sleeve. 'What will happen to his animals now? Who will look after them?'

Max put his arm around his son. 'We talked about this Tommy. We will keep checking on them, like we have been, until Fred's family decide what to do. One of Fred's children or grandchildren may choose to live there, and they'll look after the animals then.'

'But will they do it like he wanted? Fred explained it all to me, how to do it just the way he wanted. What if they don't look after them properly?' Now Meggie could see what was upsetting Tommy, he was worried for the animals.

Max took over. 'I think Fred, Mr Saunders, will have trained his children and grandchildren to look after the animals his way, just like he showed you. They'll be fine Tommy.'

Meggie watched as Tommy digested this, then gave his father a half smile. 'Okay. And we'll still look after them for now too.' Max nodded and Tommy was appeased, instantly segueing to food. 'Can we turn the oven on now? I'm hungry.'

'Turn it on to 200 degrees and you can set the table while it heats up.' Tommy shot off toward the kitchen and Max turned to Meggie, speaking more softly, 'Sometimes he takes a while to process; likes to hear the facts a couple of times.'

'It's okay Max. I get it.' She stood then, walking across to the dining table. Standing there, hands-on-hips she looked at the placemats Tommy had laid out.

'I don't know Tommy. This doesn't seem right. It's Friday night.' She made her voice light and he looked at her quizzically.

'I like to eat pizza on my lap on Friday nights, while I watch a movie.' She waited, delighted when his face lit up.

He turned to Max to check. 'Can we Dad? Eat on the sofa and watch a movie?'

Max laughed. 'Sure mate. Meggie says it's okay. Why don't

you pick a movie.' Max looked at his watch. 'One that goes for 90 minutes or so, because then we can watch the footy after, if Meggie doesn't mind.'

NEXT AFTERNOON THEY DROVE OUT TO DRUM'S PLACE. MEGGIE was a bit nervous, but Harriet had seemed brighter when they spoke that morning and said she was genuinely looking forward to the event.

The children ran around in the front yard as evening began to close in, while the meat sizzled on the barbecue and salads were fine-tuned. They fed the kids first, little Charlie and Warwick eating sausages and potato salad with the older children before they retired to the family room to watch a movie. Tiffany, Tommy and Billie seemed happy to keep an eye on the little ones, while their parents sat around Drum's large dining table.

The conversation flowed, and Meggie noticed that Rose now had a noticeable baby bump, which she patted gently from time to time. Melanie was glowing too, and Meggie knew she'd told Angus and Rose about her pregnancy earlier in the week, and Debbie and Jamie. Both women radiated good health and happiness and Meggie had a momentary pang of envy. However, deep in her heart, she knew her time would come. Knew she'd have a baby with Max. One day. But she hoped it would be sooner rather than later.

She saw Harriet look at Debbie, then both began clearing the table. Meggie got up to help but not before she saw Jamie give Debbie a concerned look.

In moments the five women were in the kitchen, some

getting the desserts out while the others rinsed plates and packed the dishwasher, chatting generally about the dinner, the children, their men. Standing at the sink with Debbie, Meggie asked quietly, 'Is everything okay Deb? Jamie just gave you a look.'

Debbie sighed, then chuckled. Wiping her hands on a tea towel, she peered into the dining area where the men were in deep conversation about the benefits of lucerne crops.

'Rose knows, and Harriet and I were talking this week. It's not a big deal, really, but I'd like to bring you up to speed too.' Debbie's look included Melanie and Meggie. 'You know I had a rough time having Woz, my pregnancy was high risk.' Rose stepped closer to Debbie, slipping an arm around her waist and Meggie marvelled again at the strength of their friendship. 'Jamie and I have decided we won't risk another pregnancy. But we'd like another child. We're looking into adoption.' Her eyes shone as she spoke, and Meggie felt a bubble of happiness rise in her chest. How beautiful.

She was keen to learn more, but Angus appeared in the doorway. 'The little ones are ready for bed. Jamie's putting Woz in the porta-cot in the spare room. I think Charlie will be alright in the bed there too. What do you think Rose?'

Rose nodded. 'It's your turn Angus Hamilton. But I've got your back if he escapes.' They all laughed. Little Charlie Hamilton was notorious.

'I've got Billie and Tiffany on my team. They assure me they can get him settled.' Angus retreated and his laughter could be heard as he walked down the hall.

Melanie looked at Meggie. 'What do you think Tommy is doing while the girls try their hand at baby-sitting?'

'Hmm. That's easy. He'll be at the dining table waiting for

dessert. The boy likes his food.' Meggie giggled as Rose peeked into the next room.

Returning, Rose was bent double, tears streaming down her face. 'Stop! Too funny. He is. At. The table.' She had a hand between her legs, and still laughing began to duck-walk from the room. 'Need. To. Pee.'

The women looked at each other and laughed. Harriet sidled up to Meggie and nudged her with her shoulder. 'Women friends. We need women friends in our lives.' She nudged Meggie again. 'Like you Meggs.'

Meggie, laughing too, wiped her eyes with a tissue, trying not to smudge her mascara. Rose returned to the room and let out an exaggerated sigh of contentment, which set them off on another bout of giggling.

Drum called from the other room, laughter in his voice. 'We have people here. Waiting for dessert!'

Tiffany assured Rose that Charlie was asleep, just like little Warwick. Drum told the kids they could take their dessert into the other room and watch a movie. They took their plates and bolted, before anyone changed their minds.

'It's really lovely to have you all here. At table together, thank you.' Meggie thought Drum's words seemed oddly formal. Harriet lay down her fork, although she'd barely touched her cheesecake.

'You know my history.' Harriet looked at each of them. Meggie found herself nodding. 'I've been experiencing some pain. And other symptoms.' Harriet smiled at Meggie. 'Two weeks ago, Meggie drove me to Sydney, for medical tests. I couldn't even tell Drum that I was unwell. Not until I knew what it was. I'll admit I was terrified. I couldn't have faced it without you, Meggs.'

Meggie saw the reactions on her friends' faces. Concern on all, except Drum's. Good. He knew what was coming. Meggie wished she did. She reached for Max's hand. He held it firmly as Harriet continued.

'Cancer or endometriosis seemed the most likely result. A full week of testing didn't turn up anything conclusive. Yet I still had pain. Finally, I had an ultrasound.' She took a breath. 'We found a mass.' Rose and Melanie paled, Debbie took a deep breath.

Harriet was leaning into Drum. Meggie couldn't take her eyes off her friend's pale face. She had circles under her eyes. 'That mass. Has a heartbeat. I'm pregnant.'

Meggie closed her eyes for a moment. Drum was still holding Harriet tightly, who looked about to cry.

Drum spoke. 'Harri was told, after the stabbing, that she wouldn't be able to bear a child. Too much scarring. Harri took this to mean she couldn't fall pregnant.' He grinned then. 'Obviously not the case. Or my guys are just super swimmers.'

It seemed everyone began to speak at once, the girls were hugging Harriet, the men pumping Drum's hand. Then Drum raised his hand, asking for quiet. 'The thing is, Harri is pregnant. Possibly ten or twelve weeks. The pain she's had is to do with everything expanding. The scarring is still an issue.' He took a breath. 'It's unlikely she can carry to full term. But if we can get close to thirty weeks, we can elect for a c-section.'

Harriet spoke then, her words carried a note of authority. 'Longer than thirty weeks, if we can.' Meggie liked their use of 'we'. Drum was totally invested. 'I'd like to get to thirty-six weeks. I'll be monitored closely. We're hoping for the best. But it's by no means a sure thing.'

Drum seemed to change the subject suddenly, perhaps to

give Harriet a moment to catch her breath. He turned to Meggie. 'I've been meaning to tell you that I'm on board with the new business, the elopement ceremonies. Even with Harriet working a bit less, you can use Melrose.'

Meggie blinked, surprised by the sudden change of pace. 'Thank you Drum. That's great news.' She watched as he stood, dragged Harriet's chair out from the table a bit. Dropping to one knee in front of her, he pulled a small box out of his pocket.

'Harriet Russell. Will you marry me?' He opened the box, Meggie could see a solitaire diamond on a rose-gold band, sparkling bright.

Harriet bit her bottom lip, her voice uncertain. 'But Drum. What if, what if..?' Her eyes filled with tears.

'Harriet. It's not about the baby, although I couldn't be happier. It's about you. I thought I was losing you. I love you. I want you here, with me and Billie. Always.' He placed his hand gently on her stomach. 'And this little guy too. We'll take that one day at a time. Together.'

Meggie felt tears coursing down her own cheeks and heard Rose sniffle as Angus passed her a handkerchief.

Melanie leaned forward. 'He needs an answer Harri. Just tell him how you feel.'

Harriet held her hand out, letting Drum slide the ring onto her finger. 'Yes! My answer is yes. I love you Drum, so much.'

'Excellent. Great. So happy.' He kissed her hard on the mouth and the room erupted with cheers and laughter.

Drum turned to Meggie. 'How quickly can you organise an elopement wedding? Here. All of us. Harriet's family. Maybe a few others. Not too much fuss.'

Meggie looked from Drum to Harriet. Her friend was

nodding vigorously. 'Yes Meggie. First elopement. Here. I say three weeks. Four at most.'

Feeling the tension of the last two weeks leave her shoulders, Meggie laughed. 'I can pull it together in two weeks, if you want. It will be the most beautiful elopement. Ever.' She moved closer to Harriet, enveloping her in a tight hug.

Melanie looked around. 'Wait! Rose. Me. Harri. We're all due within weeks of each other. What's going on? There must be something in the water!' The room rang with laughter and Meggie felt a whirlpool of longing, deep within her.

Max's breath was against her ear. She expected him to whisper something. But he surprised her. Leaning back, he spoke loud enough for them all to hear. 'Meggie, darling. Can I get you a glass of water?'

EPILOGUE

Max straightened his tie and looked over Tommy's head at Meggie. Her face was sombre, and Tommy's hand had slipped inside hers. The last funeral Tommy attended had been his mother's and Max worried it would bring the pain of that time back to him. But he was focussed on the activity at the front of the church, the service finished, the pall-bearers now lifting the coffin to their shoulders.

They stood as the procession passed by, heading to the hearse parked outside. There would be no graveside service, Fred had chosen cremation, so the mourners were heading out to the farm for the wake. Tommy had been keen to go, and Max knew he wanted to check the animals. They hadn't been out there for a few days; the house was full of Fred's children and grandchildren.

'You can take your jacket off Tommy, put your rugby jumper on instead.' Meggie was standing by the car at the farm and

Max watched her help Tommy change. She even had his gumboots ready for him to slip into. He loved her mothering instincts. 'You can head straight around to the animals but take your boots off before you come inside for afternoon tea.'

'Thanks Meggie, I will.' She winked at him, and Max watched Tommy take off through the front yard and around the side of the house. Meggie lifted out the blueberry cheesecake she'd made that morning before walking toward the house together.

Meggie murmured something and he leaned toward her to hear what she said. 'Sorry Meggie, didn't catch that.'

Meggie had stopped at the gate to the front yard. She looked at the house, its chamferboard walls and corrugated iron roof, then back to Max. 'It's really pretty. Bigger than Harriet's cottage but has similar lines.'

'Same era, I expect. And Fred has looked after it. The exterior was painted just a few years ago.' They walked up the path together, greeting Sally, then Jake as they went inside. They'd spoken to the family at the church, but it had been a large funeral, Fred was well-known in the district, and respected.

Max spent some time speaking to Drum, Ben and Angus, and he noticed Meggie was with Rose and Melanie, and some of the family in the kitchen. Tommy had come in for afternoon tea, then out again with Samantha, Fred's granddaughter. She was much older than Tommy. Playing with the puppies, no doubt.

Jake asked for quiet and said a few words, thanking everyone for coming and especially those who had helped in recent months as their father's health declined. He singled out Max and Tommy, although he was still outside, for their care of Fred's animals too.

After that people started to drift away and Drum left with Angus and Rose. Max strolled over to Meggie. 'We might head off soon.' As she nodded her agreement, Ben appeared.

'Excuse me Max. Sally and Jake have asked if you'll have a word with them. They're in Fred's study. I think it's about their plans for the livestock.'

'Wait a moment, Meggie, I'll just go and speak to them quickly.' Max followed Ben through the house.

Sally stepped forward when he entered the study, the room was filled with Fred's children and a couple of the older grand-children. She hugged Max quickly and checked that he knew everyone. Ben remained near the open door, leaning against the door jamb, his head almost touching the top of the door-way, a strange expression on his face.

'We want to thank you for everything you, and Tommy, have done for Dad. He spoke of you often and your daily visits were the highlight of his day.' Jake's words were warm, but Max was embarrassed, he'd been thanked enough.

'Except for my Friday visits!' Sally smiled, nudging her brother in the ribs. Max looked around the room at Fred's family. Having spoken to each of them since Fred's death, he knew they were happy he died peacefully and painlessly, at home as he wanted.

'Max,' Jake spoke again, and Max returned his focus. 'Dad told us he promised a puppy to Tommy, and he can take his pick. We understand he plans to follow in your footsteps Max and become a Vet. Dad told us that more than once, too.'

Max chuckled. 'He's certainly keen enough. And deter-mined too.' He loved hearing that Fred had spoken proudly of Tommy. 'Thank you. For the puppy. Tommy doesn't know about the puppy agreement, but I'll tell him later today. He'll be very excited.' Max began to say thank you to them, and take his leave, but Sally spoke up.

'There's one other thing Max.' He turned back to her.

'Dad had hoped one of us might take over the house, and the farm. We've discussed it a lot and told Dad, before he died, that it was unlikely to happen. We're all settled, and the grand-kids have other plans.' Max nodded at Sally's words, his mind beginning to whirl with possibility.

'We're placing the property on the market.' She looked at Ben. 'With Ben. But Dad asked us to offer it to you first Max, before it was listed. He discussed it with Ben and set a price too. It's a walk-in, walk-out price, including all stock and equipment, even most of the furniture. We're just going to take his personal effects.'

Max, shocked, looked at Ben, who stepped forward. 'It's a fair price Max. Come down to the office in the morning and I'll take you through it. If you, and Meggie, are happy we can go to contract.'

Max was struggling to find appropriate words, and as Sally hugged him and the others pumped his hand he looked at Ben. 'Can you find Meggie, bring her in?'

Minutes later, Meggie, looking bemused, joined them in the study. The family outlined their offer again and Max watched Meggie's face closely as she digested it.

'Really?' She spoke quietly, but Max knew they all heard. The room had gone quiet. 'It's so.' She stopped, gulped. 'Pretty. And perfect. It's just perfect for us.' She threw her arms around Max, then Sally. He knew then, it was the right time. Tommy had returned, was standing with Ben, wondering what the fuss was about.

'Come here son, we need to ask Meggie something.' Tommy

wove through the adults to stand beside Max. 'Meggie, the Masters' men would like to ask you ...' He could see tears forming in her eyes. 'If you'll become a Masters too?'

There was cheering, someone let out a 'whoop' and he thought he heard Sally say, 'Dad would be so happy right now,' but his only focus was on Meggie. She moved into his arms, kissed him, then knelt, pulling Tommy into a tight hug. 'I will. I will become a Masters too.'

Max watched Tommy's face light up. *Wait 'til they tell him about the puppy!*

THE END

ACKNOWLEDGMENTS

My thank you's always start with my girls, Jasmine and Emily. Without your encouragement, support (and marketing advice), this book would never have been completed. I love you and your little people, Edmund and Olive.

And Bloke. Thank you for the medium-rare barbecue steaks, chicken schnitty's and morning omelettes. A writer needs sustenance. But more than that - thank you for being a rich source of memes, Bloke-isms (some of which made it into the story, so now you have to read it), and most of all your absolute certainty that my words will find readers.

Huge thank you to my writing posse; Rhonda Forrest, Louise Forster, Leanne Lovegrove and Emma Powell. Love our Zoom chats, writing support, editing assistance and the sharing of marketing intel. We started this journey on spec - who would have thought, when I first made contact in Sept 2020, that we'd be writing our third book in the Love in A Sunburnt Land series in 2023? I'm in it for the long-haul girls.

Thank you to my friend and photographer - Angie White of *@photographybyangiewhite* for the stunning cover images. So many to choose from. You're a superstar! Plus a big shout-out to cover models Nathan Storer and Ted. I'm not sure which of you is cuter!

ABOUT THE AUTHOR

A voracious reader, Susan dreamed of becoming a writer from the age of eight. Career advisors told her it wasn't a real thing and suggested journalism. So she became a journalist, then took a zig-zag path to publish her first book in 2020, via a varied career in publishing, marketing, tourism and small business. Susan even worked in State Government for a few years (but she doesn't talk about that much).

Nervous about the release of Charlie's Will, she told Bloke while sitting on the sofa one night, that she'd be happy if she sold fifty. Charlie's Will quickly reached Number One in its genre on Amazon - motivating Susan to crack on with more stories and take her writing seriously. Finally. Now Susan is a happy Indie Publisher and offers services to other writers (editing, formatting). She is also the publisher of the Love in a Sunburnt Land Anthology series, co-authored with four (quite brilliant) Aussie women.

Susan loves engaging with fellow authors and readers, and she discovered something she thought was kinda funny. A lot of authors tell her they're introverted. It's a writerly thing, apparently. But (and here's the funny bit), Susan isn't. Introverted. Not one bit. Not at all. Speaking and presenting at writers festivals, conferences and libraries is totally her thing.

So it's okay to send Susan a message, ask a question and chat on social media. She thrives on it and will always respond. Send her a photo of one of her books 'in the wild' and she'll share it. Everywhere.

www.susanmackie.com

ALSO BY SUSAN MACKIE